dog

A NOVEL BY SNEED B. COLLARD III

sense

Ω
Published by
PEACHTREE PUBLISHERS
1700 Chattahoochee Avenue
Atlanta, Georgia 30318-2112

www.peachtree-online.com

Cover design by Loraine M. Joyner
Book design by Melanie McMahon Ives

Manufactured in United States of America

10 9 8 7 6 5 4 3 2 (hardcover)
10 9 8 7 6 5 4 3 2 1 (trade paperback)

Library of Congress Cataloging-in-Publication Data

Collard, Sneed B.
  Dog sense / by Sneed B. Collard III.-- 1st ed.
     p. cm.
  Summary: After he and his mother move from California to Montana to live with
his grandfather, thirteen-year-old Guy gradually adjusts to the unfamiliar surround-
ings, makes a friend, and learns to deal with a bully, with the help of his Frisbee-
catching dog, Streak.
  ISBN 13: 978-1-56145-351-1 / ISBN 10: 1-56145-351-X (hardcover)
  ISBN 13: 978-1-56145-460-0 / ISBN 10: 1-56145-460-5 (trade paperback)
  [1. Dogs--Fiction. 2. Bullies--Fiction. 3. Schools--Fiction. 4. Moving, Household--
Fiction. 5. Grandfathers--Fiction. 6. Montana--Fiction.] I. Title.
  PZ7.C67749Dog 2005
  [Fic]--dc22
                                        2005010821

dog

A NOVEL BY SNEED B. COLLARD III

sense

PEACHTREE
ATLANTA

Acknowledgments

Howls of gratitude go out to the many mammals who inspired and helped me write this book. Major "Aaaooooos" to my writer's group—Dorothy, Bruce, Jeanette, Peggy, Hanneke, and Wendy—who helped me chew the first chapters into shape. Jennifer Walworth, Mark Kayll, and my father Sneed B. Collard Jr. also spent extensive time reading, commenting, and slobbering over the manuscript. A good back scratch to my wife Amy for helping me with the counselor scene. My editor, Vicky Holifield, provided essential expertise and ideas to help me get to the marrow of the story. Lastly, there wouldn't have been a story without my wonderdog Mattie. Her keen intelligence, Olympic athleticism, and sense of humor provided not only the idea for the story, but its heart and soul. Woof! Woof!

For Mattie,
the best dog a boy could ask for.
AAA-OOOooooooo!
—S. B. C.

Chapter One

My body hits the wall like a feed sack. My head smacks the stone and I hear ringing in my ears. Then one of the ugliest faces I've ever seen appears in front of me. The boy—he looks more like a gorilla—weighs at least twice my 120 pounds and the grin on his face spreads wider than a jack-o'-lantern's. His crooked nose almost touches mine. He's so close my eyes can barely focus, but I can make out a scar running across his left eyebrow and several whiskers poking like hog bristles from his chin and upper lip.

"Welcome to B. S. Middle School," he spits. His breath hits me like volcanic sulfur, and even though my body is trembling, I find myself wondering what kind of rotten meat he's been feeding on.

"What do you want?" I ask, trying to smooth the quaver in my voice. From behind Sulfur Breath, I hear mean-sounding chuckles from a couple of guys who are obviously part of the welcoming committee. I glance over the gorilla's shoulder to see that one of them is tapeworm skinny, stands about six feet tall, and wears a dirty red National Rifle Association baseball cap on his head. The other lurks like a maggot. He's short, has bad teeth, and looks more than a little unhappy about the gene pool evolution has handed him.

"You the new California kid?" Sulfur Breath hisses.

"Yeah, I'm from California."

"Then what I want is your nuts in a vise. I *hate* Californians, so don't do anything to piss me off. You understand?"

I try to hold his gaze, but he presses me harder against the stone. His forearms feel like steel as they drive into my chest. I look away.

"Yo comprendo," I say.

"What?" he says, slamming me into the wall again. "This is America, got it? We speak English here. Not no friggin' Italian."

"I understand. I get it," I say, not bothering to point out I'd been speaking Spanish.

With one last shove he says, "Good." The two parasites in tow, he lumbers off in search of his next prey item.

"Geez," I mutter, checking my shirt for blood. "If he needs to mark his territory, why doesn't he just pee on the building or something?"

"Aw...don't worry about him. He does that to all the new kids."

I glance up to see a lanky, sandy-haired kid watching me. The zits on his face look like they're holding a convention.

"I'm Luke Grant," he says, holding out his hand. This kind of throws me, because no one shakes hands in California.

I put out my hand. "Guy."

Now he looks confused.

"That's my name," I tell him. "Guy Martinez. Guy is a family name."

"Oh," Luke says, but then he studies me for a moment. "You don't look Mexican. Isn't Martinez a Mexican name?"

"Spanish," I correct him. "My great-great-great-grandfather came over from Spain."

"Aw...you don't look Spanish, either."

"I'm not. I'm from California."

"Oh," Luke replies, apparently satisfied. "You an eighth grader?"

"Yeah."

"Me too. Maybe we'll have some classes together."

Just what I need, I think. I nod toward the T-rex who slammed me against the wall and ask, "Who's Sulfur Breath?"

"That's Brad Mullen. He's just a jerk. Stay out of his way and you'll do okay."

"What's his problem?" I ask.

"Hey," Luke exclaims. "Look at that cool dog!"

My head snaps around just in time to see my Border collie Streak dash in front of a honking school bus and bolt across the street into a crowd of students.

"Crap," I moan, rushing toward him. "Streak, come!"

Happily wagging his stump of a tail, Streak dances and darts from one group of kids to another, sticking his nose in crotches, licking backpacks, and nipping at people's shoelaces. Some of the kids squeal or laugh. One girl shouts, "Get away, you mutt!" I give my special two-note whistle before Streak can give Brad Mullen a butt sniff. Streak hears the whistle and lopes over to me.

"Is that *your* dog?" Luke asks.

"Yeah," I sigh, clutching Streak's collar. "He's mine."

Just then the eight o'clock school bell blares across the school grounds. Streak lets out a long howl in sympathy and all the kids around me laugh. I can feel my face turning red. "I've got to take him home," I tell Luke.

"You'll be late."

Let's all state the obvious.

* * *

It's hard to believe, but my day actually started out okay. Mom made me pancakes to set a positive tone for my first day at a new school in a new town in a new state. Grandpa snored his way through breakfast, allowing me to get ready in peace. As I strolled the four blocks between Grandpa's house and the school, I had actually said to myself, "Well, maybe Montana won't be such a bad place to live after all."

Right.

Now, only fifteen minutes later, I've already become

a target for a homicidal bully and my dog has escaped Grandpa's backyard and followed me to school.

I hear the second school bell ring behind me. "Well, you dummy," I say, looking down at Streak. "It's official. I'm late for my first day of school."

Streak wags his stump and jumps up on me.

"Off!" I say, gently kneeing him in the chest. "Don't try to make up with me. You are a *bad dog!*"

Streak's ears go back and I immediately regret yelling at him. I've read that Border collies are especially sensitive and you can't bawl them out too much or they turn schizo. "Oh, it's okay," I tell him and give his head a good rub.

My mom got Streak for me right after we moved to Montana—part of a guilt-induced payoff for making me leave all my friends and move to the end of the known solar system. I think she also thought a pet would help take my mind off of Dad's unannounced departure a year ago. A few days after we got here, she spotted Streak's picture in the local paper under "Mutt of the Week" and said, "Guy, I think we need a dog."

I'd never really thought about it, but the next day she drove Grandpa and me down to the Coffee County Humane Society. When they let Streak out of his kennel, the first thing he did was pee on the kennel-keeper's foot. That sold me. I didn't care that his tail had been lopped off. I just laughed and said, "I want him."

In retrospect, I should have predicted that Streak would pee on some of Grandpa's furniture, too, but fortunately he only ruined one old chair before I got him housebroken. Grandpa took it pretty well.

I jog the last block to Grandpa's house, Streak trotting along beside me. When we reach the front porch, I wonder how I'm going to keep Streak from following me to school again. "You can't come with me, okay?" I tell him.

Streak looks up with his intense chestnut eyes and I notice again what a handsome dog he is. His black coat gleams in the sunlight. A white ring spreads around his neck and down his chest, and one lightning bolt of white fur runs over his head and down his nose. That's why I named him Streak, but it could have been for his lightning speed. As he looks up at me, I can tell that all he wants right now is a good game of chase-the-ball.

"No game," I say. "We'd better put you inside for the day." I ease open the front door, trying not to make any noise.

"Guy, is that you?" Grandpa calls from upstairs.

I glance back at Streak and whisper, "Now look what you've done."

"Guy?" my grandfather yells again.

"It's me, Grandpa!" I shout, wondering if he's got his hearing aid in yet. Not that I really think he needs it. When he wants to, he seems to hear a lot of things— like front doors opening, for instance.

"Bring me up a glass of V8, would you, son?"

"Okay!"

I walk to the kitchen and pour a glass of the thick, blood-red liquid. When I get upstairs, my grandfather is sitting up in his bed adjusting the tiny volume knob on his hearing aid. I hand him his drink.

"Thank you, son." He takes a big slurp and sets the glass down, a bright ring of crimson painting his upper lip. I shudder. You couldn't pay me to drink that stuff.

Then Grandpa asks, "How was school today?"

I roll my eyes. Sometimes right when he wakes up, Grandpa acts a little confused, but this time I think he's faking it to keep the conversation going.

"Grandpa," I say. "I haven't *been* to school yet. I'm late and have to go."

"Oh? Well, you'd better get crackin'. In my day when we were late, the teacher gave us the shoe!"

Not daring to ask what "the shoe" is, I hurry out of the room. "Good-bye, Grandpa!"

I'm only halfway down the stairs when I hear his voice again. "Guy?"

I sigh and stop. "Yeah?"

"My 'roids are actin' up again. Can you get me my 'H'?"

Oh man, I think, not the hemorrhoids again. Reluctantly I hop back up the stairs and head to the bathroom. I look in the medicine cabinet, but the white-and-blue tube isn't there.

"Where is it?" I shout.

"Where's what?"

"Your Preparation H!"

"Look in the drawer."

I can pretty much guarantee it's not going to be in the drawer, but I open it anyway and, surprise, there's the tube—lying right on top of my toothbrush. Even better, the tube's cap is missing and some of the yellow ointment has leaked out onto the toothbrush bristles.

"Oh, gross," I mutter.

"What?"

"Nothing!" Grimacing, I dangle the tube between my thumb and forefinger and walk it in to Grandpa.

"It won't bite you! It's just Prep H," Grandpa tells me.

"Yeah, I know," I mumble, already planning to buy a new toothbrush after school. Before Grandpa can ask me to actually *help* him with the Preparation H, I rush down the stairs and out of the house.

Chapter Two

I run all the way back to school, even though I know it makes no sense. I'm late, so I might as well take my time and enjoy it. But I can't. I'm a worrier. Mom says Dad was a worrier, too. He just worried all the time about everything—losing his job, getting in car accidents, catching fatal diseases, and almost anything else you can think of. But I think it went deeper than that.

When I was younger, everything seemed fine. We had fun together and joked around a lot. As I got older, though, Dad started keeping to himself more and more. Once I found him sitting in the garage alone, tears streaming down his face. I asked him what was the matter, figuring I'd done something wrong, but he just wiped his face and shook his head. Several times I overheard Mom say Dad was "depressed" when she didn't know I was listening. I thought she meant he was unhappy, but looking back, I think he was Depressed with a capital *D*. Depressed as in sick.

I think Mom tried to get him help, but it didn't work.

One day about a year ago, I woke up and he was just gone.

Of course, Mom's never been depressed a day in her life—at least not that I know about. Even after my dad left, she seemed sad, but she just kept going like everything was going to work out. I don't know how she does that. Take today, for instance.

It isn't working out at all.

Hurrying down the street, I see Big Sky Middle School loom ahead of me for the second time today. The school is a two-story beige stone building with the date 1928 chiseled into the corner foundation. I figure it must have been built about the same time Coffee became a town. Of course, Coffee isn't a *real* town. People here think it's the New York City of the West with its population of 8,000 people and three grocery stores to choose from. Not me. It feels more like 80 people live here, not 8,000, and they all seem to look and act the same.

Climbing the school's front steps, I pull the comb from my pocket and run it through my hair. I don't know why I bother. Combing my black hair just makes it get wilder. It's like it has anti-gravity molecules that make it float up toward the stratosphere. And even if I *could* make my hair submit, it wouldn't make me any better looking than I was yesterday or the day before. I'd still have the same boring brown eyes, big nose, and whiskerless face. The same average build that no self-respecting girl would glance at twice.

But when I slide the comb back into my pocket, I

suddenly realize that I have a more immediate problem than my looks. To my horror, I discover that I'm no longer carrying my backpack and the Lakers jacket Mom got me for my thirteenth birthday. I know I had them when I left for school the first time. *Where are they?* I ask myself. *Did I leave them back at Grandpa's house?*

Then I remember. I dropped them when Brad Mullen slammed me against the wall.

I take a quick look around the front of the school for my lost possessions, but they are definitely Missing in Action. Crap. Mom and I barely have enough money to buy stuff like books and notebooks. There's no way I'll replace that jacket. To top it off, I now have to go to the school office and explain why I'm late.

* * *

As I'm telling the school secretary about Streak and Grandpa and everything else that's happened this morning, a man in a gray suit comes up behind her and says, "You're Guy Martinez, aren't you?"

"Yeah," I say, staring at the gleaming yellow Donald Duck tie around his neck.

A large hand appears. "Welcome to Big Sky Middle School," the man says.

Again with the hand-shaking. What is it with this place? I pump the hand a couple of times and say, "Thanks. I just need a pass to go to my homeroom."

"You're from California, aren't you?"

"Yeah. Santa Barbara."

"Well, I need to explain a few things about this school to you. First of all, children address adults as 'sir' and 'ma'am' here at Big Sky. Do you understand?"

I can feel my heart pick up speed. This isn't chitchat. This is a lecture. Why didn't I see it coming?

"Yeah...I mean, yes sir."

"Good. Also, we *all* have reasons we could be late every day. Maybe my coffeepot broke. Maybe a good song was on the radio. Maybe I just felt like sleeping a little longer."

"But this wasn't a—"

The man holds up his hand. "It doesn't matter *what* the reason is. Late is late. And here at Big Sky, we don't tolerate late. You understand?"

"Yes...sir."

"By the way, my name is Principal Goode, with an *e*. Mrs. Bellweather, please give Guy here a note so he can get to class. And welcome to Big Sky, Guy."

"Thanks...I mean, thank you...sir."

Some welcome, I think, walking down the long hallway toward my homeroom. By now I'm totally freaked and the long hallway doesn't help. Just walking down an indoor hallway creeps me out. In my school in California, all of the walkways were outside with overhangs. I wish it was like that here, but maybe I'll feel differently in February.

I stop outside my homeroom and take a deep breath. Opening this door is one more thing I'm not looking forward to today, but I muster my courage and turn the handle. As I walk in, twenty-eight eighth-grade faces turn to look at me. A primeval shudder cascades down my spine. I force myself to walk up to the teacher, a small, blond-haired woman.

"Hello," she says, turning to me. "My name is Mrs. Minneman."

As she says her name, all I can think of is Mini Me from the Austin Powers movies.

"Hi," I say, handing her my note. "I mean, hello, ma'am."

Fortunately, she doesn't bless me with the same lecture I got from the principal. All she says is "We're starting in on our first book, Guy. Please take a seat over there."

"Over there" happens to be right next to Luke—the tall dweeb I met before school. I'm going to run out of the room screaming if he tries to shake my hand again. Instead, as I near my seat he holds up my backpack and Lakers jacket. "I picked these up for you. I thought you might want them."

Relief floods through me. I wonder if this is how Grandpa feels when he uses his Preparation H.

"Thanks," I tell Luke, almost calling him "sir."

"As I was saying," Mrs. Minneman tells us, "literature is an adventure. That's why I use it to teach English. You've all had English classes before, but as eighth graders you get to start *using* what you've learned. And that is the whole point of education. I'm here not only to help you strengthen your reading and writing skills, but to help you *enjoy* those skills. And there's no better way to do that than to read good books."

I stifle a moan. I hate reading. What I mean is, I

hate reading *fiction.* My mom devours novels. She gets up early in the morning before work, makes herself a pot of coffee, and reads—sometimes for an hour or more. I don't know what she gets out of it. I mean, I like to check out sports scores in the newspaper, and I read books about animals and things like that. But every time my mom or a teacher gives me a novel, by the third paragraph I feel like someone's planted an ice ax in my brain. *But maybe,* I tell myself, *this teacher will give us some good nonfiction for a change.*

"The first novel we're going to explore," Mrs. Minneman says, "is a newer book that's already becoming a classic. It's one that boys should especially like."

I groan inside.

"The book's title is *The Watsons Go to Birmingham—1963* by Christopher Paul Curtis."

I've never been to Birmingham, but already I know I'm going to hate this book. How? Because well-meaning English teachers and librarians have been feeding me books "for boys" since I was in fourth grade, and I've hated every single one of them.

But Mrs. Minneman has to do her duty. She passes us each a copy, explaining our assignment as she goes. "Your homework is to read this book by the end of the week and write a two-page description of what you thought about it and why—due on Monday. Are there any questions?"

Yeah, I think. *When do I turn eighteen so I can get out of here?*

* * *

14

After English, things look like they're getting better. I go to social studies and Spanish, both of which I like all right. Then I have P.E., but since it's the first day, we don't have to dress in our gym clothes. At lunch I manage to find a corner table where no one bothers me, and after that I have typing—or "keyboarding." When I walk out of there, all I have left is math, and that's my best subject.

Home free, I tell myself.

Right.

When I walk into class, the first thing I see is Sulfur Breath and the Parasites. My brain goes numb. When the neurons start firing again, I wonder if I'm in the wrong room.

"Well, look who's here," Brad Mullen sneers. "It's the California Kid. Or should I say the Calf-Crap Kid?" This witticism draws a chorus of guffaws from Tapeworm and Maggot. Brad motions toward an empty desk on his row. I hesitate for a moment, but then I spot Luke. Grateful for anything resembling a friendly face, I walk over and take the desk in front of him. I pull out a pencil and start tapping the eraser on the desk.

"Hey, Calf Crap," Sulfur Breath says. "I want you sittin' over here."

Fortunately, before I have to respond, a tall, gaunt teacher wearing a rumpled suit walks in. His pasty gray face looks tired. Not the I-didn't-get-enough-sleep-last-night kind of tired. He looks tired of *life.* "I'm Mr. Krauss," he says. "This is Math Foundations."

I stop tapping the pencil.

Did he say math *foundations?*

"Welcome," Mr. Krauss says. "And for those of you who are returning, welcome again." As he says this, he takes a pointed look at Brad Mullen, but Mullen doesn't flinch.

"Hi again, Mr. Krauss," Brad says. "I liked your class so much last year, I decided to take it again."

Tapeworm and Maggot laugh and even Mr. Krauss manages a weary grin. "Let's see if we can make this your last time, Mr. Mullen. My records show that this is the only remaining class you need to pass to go to high school."

"*If* I want to go to high school," Brad says with a snort.

Mr. Krauss ignores him. "In this class," he explains, "we are going to work on math fundamentals. Let's not kid ourselves. You're not going to become math majors and I'm not Albert Einstein."

"As if you could even *play* baseball," Sulfur Breath mutters.

I roll my eyes. Albert Einstein, a baseball player? Brad definitely isn't the sharpest knife in the drawer.

Mr. Krauss continues. "Our only goal in this class is to teach you enough math skills to get you into ninth grade. We'll try to make it fun, but let's be honest here. If you don't get through this class, you are not—I repeat—*are not* going to graduate."

I can't listen any longer and raise my hand.

"Yes, Mr...." The teacher looks down at his class list.

"Martinez," I say.

"Yes, Mr. Martinez?"

"Uh, sir, I think I'm in the wrong class."

16

Mr. Krauss checks his class list again. "Oh yes. You registered late so we couldn't fit you into the advanced math program you requested."

"I didn't register late...sir."

"You didn't?"

"No sir."

"Well, did you take the placement exam?"

"What placement exam?"

"That must be the problem. If you don't take the placement exam, we can't give you a choice of classes."

Brad makes a fist. "I'll place him right now." The rest of the class laughs—all except Luke—and I feel myself getting angry.

"You mean I have to stay here?" I ask, grinding my pencil's eraser into my desk.

"Get used to it, Calf Crap," Mullen says.

"Talk to me about it after class," Mr. Krauss says. "And that's enough from you, Mr. Mullen."

Mr. Krauss hands out textbooks that look like they've been used since the Second World War. I open mine and, with growing frustration, recognize the math as stuff I had years ago—even before I had it in school. My dad was a math whiz and he worked with me from when I first started to talk, giving me flash cards and taking me through all kinds of math problems, always ahead of my school classes. I loved it. That's one of the things I miss most about my dad, sitting together working on math. I still don't understand why he couldn't solve his own problems with my mom and me, but as Grandpa says, that's smoke up the chimney.

While Mr. Krauss explains a third-grade math concept, I try to keep from melting down. Instead I start working on how I'm going to get out of this stupid class. Not only will I be wasting my time if I stay here, but I'll be a walking target for Brad Mullen. I admit it's kind of nice being in a class with Luke, but I'll be happy enough to ditch him if I can keep Sulfur Breath off my scent.

Finally the bell rings, and as the other kids file out, I walk up to Mr. Krauss's desk. He's looking through a notebook, but after a moment, he notices me.

"Yes?"

"You were going to tell me how I can get into a more advanced class," I say.

Mr. Krauss's eyes look blank, like they belong to a deactivated robot. Then, as if someone has pushed his Power On button, his eyes slowly focus. "Ah, right, Mr...."

"Martinez. Guy Martinez."

"Well, Mr. Martinez. All the other math classes are full."

"But I've already had all of this stuff...sir."

"This is what happens when you don't take the placement exam."

"But Mr. Krauss. I just moved here. No one even told me about the exam. Can't I take it now?"

Mr. Krauss gives this a whole two seconds of careful consideration. "I don't think that would be fair to the other students, do you?"

I try to follow his logic. "What? Why not?"

Mr. Krauss suddenly slaps the notebook closed in front of him. "Look, if you want, you can take it up with the principal. If not, I'll expect you to have the answers to the problems on page 13 ready to turn in tomorrow."

Chapter Three

I leave Mr. Krauss's class and slam my fist against a nearby locker. It makes a satisfying banging sound but does little to cool my jets. Then I spot Luke standing on the other side of the hall.

"Hey," I mutter. "What are you doing here?"

"Just waiting," he says as though it's the most natural thing in the world for him to be waiting for a person he barely knows. "I was thinking maybe you could show me your dog."

"Streak?" I ask, surprised.

"Yeah, Streak. I like that name."

He follows me as I head down the hall. "Don't you have to catch a bus or something?" I ask.

"Nah. I live over near you."

"How do you know where I live?"

Luke gives a little snort. "Everyone knows where you live."

Again, I'm surprised—and annoyed. "They do?"

He clamps a hand on my shoulder. "Sure. Everyone knows where *everybody* lives in this town. We knew the second you and your mom showed up."

I slide sideways so he has to let go of my shoulder. "Great."

"It's no big deal," Luke says. "Coffee's that kind of place. Everyone knows everybody else's business around here."

We push open the double front doors to the school and walk down the steps. I do a radar scan for Brad Mullen, but he's nowhere to be seen. Luke reads my mind.

"Don't worry. I heard Brad's got detention already. And even if he didn't, he and his friends usually hang out down at the Smoking Tree after school."

"Brad who?" I ask, pretending not to care.

"He's been held back twice," Luke goes on. "He ought to be a tenth grader, but he keeps getting in trouble and flunking his classes."

"Why's that?" I say as we cross the street.

"I don't know. My folks say Brad's dad used to beat on him a lot. That was before he got killed."

Before I can ask *how* Brad's father got killed, Luke presses ahead with the details.

"His dad used to drink a lot after work—when he could get work. He got a job as a log-peeler out at one of those log home–building places down the highway, you know?"

"Yeah," I say, even though I have no idea how you'd peel a log or why you'd even want to.

"So one day after work last winter he went to get a couple of beers with his friends. As he and his buddies were driving home, two big deer jumped in front of his truck. He missed the first one, but the road was icy

21

and he slid into the second one, a buck. The buck came through the front windshield and the antlers gored Brad's dad right through the chest, like swords or bayonets."

My stomach turns. "I get the picture."

"It happens a lot around here."

"Being gored by deer?"

Luke snorts again. "Aw...no. People hitting deer. Though I guess more than a couple of 'em are drunk. About five years ago, four of the best football players over at the high school were driving home from a game in Butte and the same thing happened. After their car hit the deer, a semi truck plowed into them from behind. All four of 'em got killed." Luke is telling me all this as if he's talking about the weather, but I never heard stories like this in California. Sure, there was the occasional gang shooting or surfer drowning, but killer deer?

"Well," I ask, before Luke can think of an even gorier story to tell, "who are those two guys Brad hangs out with?"

"Clyde Crookshank and Harold Dicks."

"Geez, with names like that, no wonder they're mean. Which one is the tall one?"

"That's Clyde. But don't worry about them. They think they're bad, but they don't ever do anything unless Brad's around. They got held back a grade, too."

"That's a shock."

"Huh?"

"Never mind."

We cross another couple of streets and can see my grandpa's house at the end of the block. It's hard to miss—a two-story Victorian with chipping blue paint and a roof that's long overdue for the landfill. Mom says it was built about 1915, but two or three hundred B.C. is more like it.

"Uh, Luke," I say, stopping. "You probably shouldn't stay too long. My grandpa's not feeling well and I don't know how he'll like having guests around."

Luke shrugs. "That's okay."

Does anything bother this kid?

* * *

When we reach the house, I see Streak tied to the tree in the backyard. Grandpa must have put him there, and I'm happy because now I won't have to take Luke inside. But when I drop my backpack on the front porch and start to walk around to the side gate, Luke asks, "Aw...can I use your bathroom?"

Great, I think. The one thing I want to avoid is going into the house and having to deal with Grandpa. But maybe Grandpa is down at the Union Club hanging out with his buddies. He hobbles down there a couple afternoons a week, and today could be my lucky day.

"Yeah, sure," I tell Luke.

I start to search my backpack for the house key and then remember for the hundredth time that in Coffee nobody locks their houses.

We walk into the front entryway and I smell that

musty old-house smell. I'd been getting used to it, but bringing a guest home, it hits me all over again. "The bathroom's up the stairs," I tell Luke, seeing no sign of Grandpa anywhere.

But before Luke takes a step, a voice booms out from the kitchen. "Guy? That you? I'm in here!"

My shoulders sag and I let my backpack clomp to the floor.

Luke follows me through the dining room and the doorway leading to the kitchen. We find Grandpa camped in his favorite spot, next to a small Formica-topped table that looks like something out of *That '70s Show.*

Grandpa's just sitting there, but I'm immediately embarrassed. He's got on his old coffee-stained, dung-colored overalls, even though a bad hip forced him to quit his job as a furnace repairman years ago. Gray wisps of hair rise like smoke from the top of his head and big thick bristles poke out of his ears and nose.

"Grandpa, this is Luke. Luke, Grandpa."

I want to save Luke from my grandfather as quickly as possible, but Luke steps up and—of course—puts out his hand. Grandpa shakes it vigorously. "Luke, boy, glad to meet you. Aren't you one of Daniel's boys? I seem to remember you working down at the hardware store."

"Aw...you're probably thinking of my father," Luke says. "He used to work down there."

"Your *father!*" Grandpa thinks about this for a second. "Yes, I suppose it would be. Damn. Pardon my Portuguese."

Luke laughs.

"Son," Grandpa says to me. "Pour me a glass of V8 juice. And get your friend something there, too."

I just want to get Luke out to the yard, but I keep my mouth shut and walk to the refrigerator. "You want anything, Luke?"

"Of course he does!" Grandpa says. "What'll it be, Luke? Guy's mom has some cranberry juice in there."

"Actually, if I could just use your bathroom, sir."

"Oh hey, I can relate to that!" Grandpa says. "That's my favorite place in the house. I call it my 'workbench'."

Grandpa breaks up at this witticism and Luke joins in laughing. I look to see if there's enough room for me to crawl into the refrigerator.

When Grandpa's cackling dies down, he tells Luke, "Head up the stairs there and the bathroom's straight ahead. But you stay away from my Preparation H, you hear? I need it to keep my butt cheeks from catching on fire."

"Grandpa!" I say. "Geez!"

But Luke snorts and says, "Don't worry, sir. I've got my own." Grandpa breaks up all over again and Luke heads towards the stairs. This situation is getting way too chummy for me.

I pour Grandpa his juice and hand it to him. "Grandpa, do you have to make jokes like that? I hardly know that kid."

"Embarrassed by your gramps?" he asks with a look of satisfaction. "Well, I was embarrassed by mine, too. Get used to it, son. And I'll tell you somethin' else. That boy Luke. He's a good one. You'd do well to make friends with him."

"I don't *need* friends," I say. "I have some back in California."

"That may be. But I've learned one thing in my twenty-nine years," Grandpa says, continuing his roll of bad jokes. "And that is, never pass up an opportunity to make a new friend. You never know when you'll need one."

When Luke comes back down, I say, "So, you want to see Streak?"

Luke's eyes flash. "Sure."

"Streak, now that's quite a dog!" Grandpa pipes in. "I seen a lot of canids in my day, but that's definitely one of the smartest—and fastest, too. Somehow he got in the house this morning, so I tied him up out back. I told you that yard wasn't dog-proof, didn't I, son?"

"Yes, Grandpa."

"You're going to want to take care of that posthaste-like. Streak's not the kind of dog to be tied to a tree. Anyhoots, go show your friend what Streak can do. Nice meetin' you, Luke."

Luke again puts out his hand. "Nice meeting you too, sir."

"Come back again any time. The door's always open."

I wince.

"Thank you, sir," says Luke. "I will."

* * *

When I open the side gate, Streak is staring intently at us. Most dogs would be yapping, trying to break their necks against the rope, but not Streak. He doesn't get excited until he knows what's going on. If I were a dog and someone tied me to a tree, I'd immediately think of the worst-case scenario. I'd be convinced that no one would ever come back to untie me and I'd be stuck out there until I starved. But Streak, he takes it moment by moment.

Grandpa has tied the rope through the ring on Streak's collar and, while Streak sits still, I untie it. As soon as I do, he bolts and does a crazy, joyous series of figure eights around the backyard.

Luke whistles. "That is one fast dog."

Streak darts in to nip my heel and I take a play-swipe at him. "Yeah," I say, smiling. "He sure is."

Luke kneels down and says, "Hey, Streak. Come."

"He's not much of a dog for petting. He lets me scratch him on the head, but—" Before I finish my sentence, Streak bounds up to Luke, gives him a quick kiss on the face, and submits to being rubbed on the chest.

"I guess he likes you," I say, a little miffed.

"You're a good dog, aren't you, boy?" Luke croons to Streak. "I love Border collies," he continues. "They're my favorite dogs, but they need a lot of attention."

"Tell me about it," I say. "I could throw the ball for him for hours and he'd still want more."

"Have you started training him yet?"

"Sure," I say. "Streak, sit!"

Streak sits and looks up at me expectantly.

"Okay, lie down!"

Streak plunks himself on the grass.

"Okay, roll 'em!"

Streak flings himself over and leaps back up to a standing position.

"Good boy!" I tell him. "Good boy!"

"That's pretty good," Luke says. "But I mean have you really started to train him?"

This remark annoys me. What's this kid want—for Streak to recite the Declaration of Independence? "Well," I say, "he can shake and he knows how to stay...sometimes."

Luke picks up a ball in the grass and throws it across the yard. Streak shoots after it and grabs it on the first bounce. "Border collies are really smart," Luke tells me. "Do you know that some can learn up to fifty different commands?"

I pretend not to be surprised. "Well, yeah."

"Not only that, but they do a lot better when they feel like they have a job. They're working dogs. That's why they don't like to be petted and fussed over too much. They want to be doing stuff all the time." Luke grabs the ball from Streak's mouth and throws it again.

I look at Luke. "How do you know so much about dogs?"

Luke shrugs. "This is Montana. Everybody knows about dogs."

I get the feeling he's dodging the question.

"I used to have some dogs," he says. "One was half Border collie."

"What happened to them?"

Luke tugs on his right earlobe. "They...um...died

28

and my parents didn't want me to get any more. At least for now."

"Oh. Sorry."

"Aw...it's okay."

I can tell I've hit a sore spot. "Well, you can play with Streak anytime."

Luke's face lights up like a sparkler. "You mean it?"

I shrug and wonder what I'm getting myself into. "Yeah. Uh, sure."

"Thanks."

Luke throws the ball for Streak a dozen more times, both of them obviously loving it. Then Luke says, "Well, I'd better go hit the books."

"What books? It's only the first day."

"I'm not much good at math."

"Yeah, but tonight's assignment's a whiz. Five minutes max."

"I'm kind of slow," Luke says, and I regret sounding so confident. "I already got held back in math once and want to make sure it doesn't happen again. Mom says I've got more of a reading and writing brain."

"Oh. We all have things we're lousy at," I say, trying to make him feel better. "For me, it's English. They never seem to read the stuff I like in school."

"Really? I love English. I can't wait to read *The Watsons Go to Birmingham* again."

"*Again?*"

Luke shrugs. "Yeah. I read it a couple years ago. It's a short book."

"Can you read it for me too?" I ask.

"Aw...sure," Luke says, grinning.

I walk him to the gate. "Well, guess I'll see you tomorrow."

Streak comes up and sticks his nose through the fence. Luke scratches it. "Bye, Streak. Don't wear Guy out."

Chapter Four

After Luke leaves, I throw the ball for Streak a few more times and then poke around the back-yard fence, trying to figure out exactly how my dog made his earlier escape. The fence is patched together with sections Grandpa must have salvaged from different places over the years. Chain link lines one side of the yard. Along the other is some kind of ancient wire fencing like people use to keep rabbits out of a garden. Along the back it's white picket, and up near the house he's rigged up a kind of metal tube and wire combination, with a rusting gate that leads in and out of the yard.

I find two possible escape routes. In one place on the side, the chain link hasn't been anchored and Streak could easily scoot under it. Grandpa has a pile of gravel next to the garage that sits on the alley, so I grab a shovel from the toolshed and throw a few shovelfuls along the loose fence bottom. Streak watches what I do with intense interest.

"That ought to keep you from getting out here," I tell him as I smooth out the gravel.

Streak has no comment.

"Now, what are we going to do about this other spot?" I ask him.

The other place I'm sure Streak can—and probably did—get out is the gate leading to the front. It's only about three and a half feet high, and even though Streak stands just a little taller than my knees, this dog has springs in his legs. When I hold up a ball or stick, he can leap so high that he's looking me straight in the face. It's a little unnerving having him suspended in air in front of me like some space dog, but I've gotten used to it.

Anyway, it's easy to see that with one small leap my dog is over the gate. It's not so easy to figure out what to do about it. As I'm studying the problem, my mom pulls up. I open the gate and Streak sprints out to greet her.

"Hi, honey," she says, closing the driver's side door to our faded red Honda Accord. The car's got over 200,000 miles on it and was built about the time George Washington crossed the Potomac. It farts and belches more than Grandpa does, but it still runs, so Mom hangs on to it. "We're going to drive this car until it rolls over and dies," she tells me again and again. I keep telling her it already has.

"How was work?" I ask, taking the grocery bag from her.

"Work was work," she says with a tired smile. "Kind

of slow, actually. The summer remodeling season's about over."

Back in California, Mom was a behavioral therapist for kids with screwed-up home lives and bad attitudes, and I guess she made pretty good money. But when we moved here, she took a minimum-wage job as an assistant in the interior design store owned by her old high school friend, Sara. I don't know why Mom didn't get another therapist job here. Sulfur Breath alone could keep her and two or three other people employed full-time. But she said she needed a change.

In fact, the whole move up here seems to be about *her* needing a change. I didn't need one. I was just beginning to get used to my dad being gone. I had friends. We lived close to the beach and I was learning how to surf. When my mom told me we were coming up here to live with Grandpa, I went ballistic. She tried to convince me that it would be fun, that I would love Montana, but I wasn't buying it. When that didn't work, she said we needed to be closer to family since we didn't have any in California. I told her she was all the family I needed. After a dozen skirmishes over three or four days, she finally threw up her hands and said, "Guy, we're going. I'm sorry you don't like it, but that's how it is." I thought about running away to try to find my dad, but in the end, I packed up my stuff and climbed into the Accord.

Anyway, Mom says the job at the design store is just until she finds something else, but I don't know what she's going to find in Coffee, unless it's at some fast-food dump like Burger Bite. As my dad used to say when we visited here, this place is deader than a damn doornail.

"How was your first day of school?" Mom asks, holding the front door open for me.

"It sucked." I see her cringe and immediately wish I'd just said it was okay. I try not to take things out on her, but sometimes it's not easy.

"It wasn't so bad, really," I backpedal as I slip past her into the living room.

"You have any trouble?" she asks, hooking a shock of her gray-streaked brown hair behind her ear. "Sara down at the store said there are some rough kids in that school."

"No," I lie, Brad Mullen lurking in my brain.

"That's good. Big Sky seems like it's as good as your school in California."

Right.

"It's okay," I tell her.

"Where's Grandpa?"

"Is that you, April?" Grandpa yells from the kitchen.

"It's me, Dad!" my mom calls back. I follow her into the kitchen with the grocery bag.

"How are you, Sweet Molasses?" Grandpa asks her.

"Oh, Dad," Mom says, leaning over to give him a hug. "You haven't called me that in years. The first time was when—"

"When you spilled molasses all over the backseat of our Chrysler," he interrupts.

"You did?" I ask.

Mom blushes, something she almost never does.

"You bet she did," Grandpa crows. "We went out to the county fair when your mom was...how old were you, April?"

"Seven," she says.

"We had a brand-new Chrysler and your grandma and I loved that car. Well, out at the fair, your mom here begged us to buy molasses from one of the stands. We told her she wouldn't like it, but she insisted. You know how strong-headed your mother can be."

"Tell me about it," I say.

"Anyhoots, we got back in the car and were driving home and I guess she tasted the molasses. The next thing we know, she's pouring the stuff all over the backseat."

"Dad, I wasn't *pouring* it on the seat," my mom protests. "I was trying to put it on some graham crackers that were bouncing around in my lap."

"Sure!" Grandpa snorts. "And I've got all my teeth, too! April, I should have taken you over my knee right then and there, but your mom stopped me. She always did have more patience than I did."

I try to picture Grandma, but I have only one image of her in my mind. I was visiting up here when I was about four years old. I don't know why, but I woke up early one morning and came out to find Grandma sitting in the kitchen reading the morning paper. When I came in, she gave me a warm, soft hug and asked, "Would you like some coffee?"

Mom and Dad had never let me drink coffee before, but I'd always thought it smelled really good. Grandma poured me a big cup and we sat at the same table

Grandpa is sitting at now. Of course, what my grandma gave me was mostly milk, but it made me feel grown up. We sat there talking and drinking coffee until everyone else got out of bed.

Now I look at my mom and Grandpa and wish that my grandmother was still here. I wonder if she could make everything feel like it did before.

Chapter Five

The next morning I still haven't figured out what to do about the gate. After taking Streak for a short walk, I leave him in the house and count on Grandpa taking him outside again later.

Arriving at Big Sky, I scan the crowd of students for Luke. I don't see him right away and am heading toward the front steps when my eyes catch movement behind a ponderosa pine. I recognize Brad Mullen and the Parasites pinning someone against the side the building. It's Luke. My heart races at the thought of having my face pummeled into squash and I begin to turn away.

But I can't.

"Crap," I mutter, starting toward them. As I approach, I see Sulfur Breath spitting words into Luke's face. Luke handles it like a storm-tested sailor, and I can tell he's been through this before.

"Good morning!" I say with fake enthusiasm. "How are you all? Discussing the math homework?"

"Back off," Brad hisses. "You're up next."

Going for the naïve approach, I say, "I thought the

math was pretty difficult. Especially the second-power polynomial. Did you guys have any trouble?"

That does it. Brad bounces Luke against the wall one more time and turns to me, his eyes blazing like molten lava. I wrestle for control of my bladder.

Brad moves in closer and gives me a shove. "I...told...you..." he says between shoves, "to...mind... your...own...business!"

"Yeah, California boy," adds Clyde, the tapeworm with the NRA cap.

"Leave him out of it," Luke says.

"It's okay," I tell Luke, wiping flecks of saliva from my face. Then, to Sulfur Breath, I say, "What are you so mad about? We didn't do anything to you."

"What would you know about it?" Mullen growls, giving me another shove. "Your friend's family almost ruined this town, and just *looking* at you makes my eyeballs hurt. We got enough problems without you and other Californians trying to Cal-i-forn-i-cate Montana."

I wonder what other Californians he's talking about. I haven't met anyone else from California since we moved here. I also wonder what he means about Luke's family, but I suspect this is a bad time to ask. I'm searching for some way to weasel out of the situation when a familiar voice booms out.

"Holding a bit of civil discourse this morning, boys?"

We all turn to see Principal Goode—with an *e*—strolling toward us. He's wearing the same suit as the day before, but he now sports a SpongeBob SquarePants tie. The tie thing must be his trademark or something. How creative.

"So, what did I miss?" he asks.

"Nothing, sir," Brad says in his sweetest T-rex voice. "Me and California here were just gettin' to know each other."

"Yes, I'm sure you were, Brad," Principal Goode replies as the first bell rings. "Now why don't you and your friends move along to homeroom."

"Yes sir," Brad replies, shooting me an I'll-get-you-later look.

I turn to leave, but the principal puts his hand on my shoulder. "Not so fast, Mr. Martinez. You want to tell me what that was about?"

"No sir. I mean, nothing...sir."

Principal Goode stares me down.

"Really," Luke pipes in. "We were just discussing the math homework that's due today."

I can see that the principal isn't buying it. "Well, boys, if you keep covering up for Mr. Mullen, I may have to put you in detention with him. And Mr. Martinez, I have to say I am not impressed with your start here so far. Your school in California may put up with this sort of shenanigans, but this is not California."

Like I hadn't noticed.

Principal Goode stares at me for another long second, then abruptly does an about-face and strides off, leaving us to our misery. I hear Luke let out a big sigh. Then, as if nothing has happened, he asks, "So, how's it going?"

How's it going? How well can it be going with Sasquatch wanting to rip out your lungs and the school principal breathing down your neck?

"Do you have to ask?" I say.

"Aw...you worried about Brad? Don't. He'll forget about us by noon."

"No way. That chip on his shoulder cuts all the way down to his spine. What's he got against Californians anyway?"

"A lot of people around here blame everything bad that happens on people from California. They're just jealous or something."

"That's stupid."

"Yeah, but some people just like blaming someone else for their problems." Luke speaks as if he knows this from personal experience, but before I can ask him about it, the second bell rings. Hoisting our packs, we walk toward our homeroom, Mrs. Minneman's first-period English class.

Luke asks, "Did you figure out how he got loose yesterday?"

"Huh?"

"Streak."

"Oh. Yeah, I think so," I say, and his question gives me an idea. "Luke, how good are you with fences?"

"You mean building them?"

"More like fixing them."

Luke shrugs. "I've mended a few. Why?"

"Can you come over to my grandpa's house after school?"

"Yeah, sure. Do I need to bring anything?"

"I don't think so."

That's good enough for Luke. I'm learning that he's not exactly the curious type. We reach homeroom and

Luke asks, "So, did you read *The Watsons Go to Birmingham* yet?"

"Nuh-uh," I say as we make our way to our desks.

"I finished it last night," Luke says.

I drop my pack next to my desk and stare at him. "You finished it? The whole thing?"

"It was only a couple hundred pages."

Which would make it about a hundred and fifty pages longer than anything I've ever read in my whole life. "Geez, you really do like reading, don't you?"

Luke shrugs again. "I guess so. It's a lot more interesting than television. I can lend you some books if you want. I've got hundreds of them."

"Uh, no thanks," I tell him, sliding into my chair. "My mom's got a book collection bigger than the Library of Congress. Hey, you don't think we're going to talk about *The Watsons Go to Birmingham* today, do you?"

Before Luke can answer, our teacher steps to the front of the room.

"Good morning, class," Mrs. Minneman chirps as we all settle in. "What a glorious day! Have you ever seen a day so beautiful?"

A couple of the kids mutter, but then I hear a clear voice exclaim, "No, Mrs. Minneman. It feels like spring today."

My head snaps toward the voice. I can't believe I didn't notice her the day before. Two rows to my right and one row forward sits a girl with shoulder-length brown hair that shines like silk, even under our classroom's fluorescent lights. She's wearing goofy red-rimmed glasses that date back to The Brady Bunch era, but beneath the red rims, she's got a face that could be in the movies. Smooth skin. Cheekbones that could belong to a princess. Thin—but not too thin—straight lips that seem ready to curve into a smile. More than her looks, though, it's the way she holds herself that catches me. She's sitting up with her shoulders back, and she looks directly at Mrs. Minneman. *What is it about her,* I wonder. But then I figure it out.

Confidence.

* * *

Mercifully, the rest of the day passes quickly and without too much pain. I manage to avoid any questions about *The Watsons Go to Birmingham.* We dress for P.E. and play soccer—a sport I didn't realize they had in Montana, but one I'm more or less okay at. I spend most of the day dreading math class and wondering if Brad will pick up where he left off with Luke and me this morning. When I walk in, though, I'm relieved to find he's not even in class. Neither are Tapeworm and Maggot, and I figure they must have cut school to torture little old ladies, blow up mailboxes, or perform some other helpful civic activity.

After school Luke goes to the office with me to see if I can get switched to another math class. I talk to the vice-principal and she's pretty nice—nicer than Mr. Krauss or Principal Goode. She looks up my transcripts and test scores from California and tells me she'll see what she can do. She adds that it might take a few days. I only hope it happens before Brad comes back to class.

After leaving the vice-principal's office Luke and I head for my grandpa's house, which I guess is mine now, too.

"Hey, Luke," I try to ask as casually as possible, "who's that girl in English?"

"*What* girl?"

"You know, the one with the red-rimmed glasses."

Luke gives me a blank look, and I wonder if he's ever thought about a girl in his life.

"You know, the one who told Mrs. Minneman what a nice day it was at the beginning of class."

Luke thinks another half second. Then recognition shoots across his face. "Oh, you mean Catherine."

I wait for more information, but Luke still isn't catching on.

"Well, what's her story?" I press.

"Her story? I don't know any story. Hey, look! There's Streak!"

I sigh, but then smile as I see my dog looking at us from under the apple tree in the backyard. His ears point straight up as usual and he watches us like the world depends on it.

I open the gate to the backyard, and Luke closes it behind him.

"How's my boy?" I croon, bending down to pet Streak, but he wants none of it. He's ready to play. I untie him and he rockets through four circuits of the backyard before bringing me a tennis ball that smells like moose turds. I wrench the ball from his mouth and fling it across the yard. When he fetches it, Luke takes over. I can see that they're both in heaven, and I let Streak chase down five or six throws before asking, "So, you said you're pretty good with a fence?"

"I didn't say I was *good,*" Luke says, accidentally tossing the ball into a tangle of rosebushes. Streak dives into the thicket like it's water and emerges with the ball in his mouth.

"Well, here's my problem," I say, walking over to the gate.

Luke follows, almost tripping over Streak, who doesn't want to give up the game. Luke laughs. "He is such a Border collie. They're so bossy."

"Yeah. Anyway—"

"I'll bet he can clear that gate like it's nothing."

"Exactly," I say, grateful I don't have to explain every detail. "The question is, what can I do about it?"

"You thought about replacing the gate?" Luke asks.

"I was hoping for something simpler."

Luke studies the gate for a moment, then looks around. "What's in that shed?"

Streak follows us into Grandpa's toolshed. Luke rummages around, finally pulling out some scraps of chicken wire, some baling wire, and a six-foot length of rebar. He hands me some wire cutters and a sledge-hammer.

Half an hour later, Luke—with my feeble assistance—has added two feet to the height of the gate. Even more amazing, it doesn't look half bad.

"Wow," I say. "I could never have figured that out."

"Aw...that was easy," says Luke, and he means it.

"I've had to throw together animal cages and fences lots of times."

"You have? How come?"

"Uh, well..." Luke stops, like he isn't sure he wants to tell me. Then he says, "Well, my dad, he's a vet."

"A war vet?"

Luke shakes his head. "A veterinarian. At least, he was."

"Wow, I didn't know that," I say. "What—"

"Anyway," he cuts me off, "that's how I know about fences. I should be getting home." Luke is opening the newly improved backyard gate when I remember the second part of the idea I'd had earlier.

"Wait. Since you helped me with the gate, I thought maybe I could help you with math. That is, if you want me to."

Luke's face brightens. "You mean it?"

"Sure. I've had a lot of this stuff already. Maybe I can give you a few pointers."

Luke looks so grateful that I shift my eyes awkwardly to look at Streak. "It's no big deal," I tell him.

"That'd be great."

Chapter Six

From then on I end up spending a lot of time with Luke. We eat lunch together and usually go to my house after school. One day I suggest we go to his house instead of mine—just for a change of pace. "I don't know," he says, tugging on his earlobe. "It's kind of messy over there."

I laugh. "Haven't you seen my room?"

I expect Luke to laugh, but his shoulders sag and he seems to crawl down inside himself. "It's probably not...a good idea."

I start to ask why, but I can see he doesn't want to talk about it.

So in the afternoons, we end up at my house. We play with Streak and do a little jawing with Grandpa. Then I help Luke with his algebra homework. Luke has a hard time grasping that x and y aren't mysterious supernatural powers. They just stand for things that aren't known. But when I tell him to think of haystacks instead of x and grizzly bears instead of y, we have just enough breakthroughs for Luke to scrape out C's on the tests.

If only I were so lucky in English. I manage to finish some of *The Watsons Go to Birmingham* and even write a two-page essay on it, but when Mrs. Minneman hands my paper back, a neatly drawn D decorates the front page. Next to the grade is a note: "I want to know what *you* think about the book, not what you think *I* think!"

I slump down in my desk, shaking my head. "Oh, man."

"How'd you do?" Luke whispers to me.

I show him the paper, at the same time noticing a large A- on the front of Luke's.

"You should have read the whole thing."

"I need CliffsNotes," I whisper back to him.

"Mrs. Minneman's on to that stuff. If you really want to be humiliated, write a paper from CliffsNotes or borrow one from the Internet. She'll make an example out of you."

"It doesn't matter," I mumble.

But it does matter. I glance over at Catherine talking to the girl next to her and think, *I'll bet anything she gets straight A's in here.*

Ever since that second day in school I've been watching Catherine. I watch her in English class. I watch her during lunch and keep an eye out for her between classes. And I've noticed she does some funny things. Like tapping her fingers, for instance. When Mrs. Minneman is speaking, Catherine taps her fingers quietly on her leg. Her fingers barely move; no one else seems to notice. At first I think she's just doing it because she's bored. Then I realize that she's actually counting the syllables coming out of our teacher's mouth. Before I know it, I'm doing it, too. On Thursday I come up with 949 syllables, and after class, I want to go up to Catherine to ask if my count matches what she got. Then I realize that if I do that, she'll know I've been watching her.

The next day during lunch I see her and a bunch of other girls sitting together on a bench. Suddenly her friends get up to go and Catherine is sitting all alone. Before I know what I'm doing, I get up and walk toward her. At the last minute, though, I veer off, a thousand reasons why I shouldn't talk to her swirling through my head.

I don't know what it is about this girl that makes me so nervous. Back in the fifth grade, I "went steady" with Debbie Foxen. We passed notes to each other and we held hands once, but I wasn't obsessed with her or anything.

Catherine's different. Every time I see her push her big red-rimmed glasses higher on her nose or tuck a strand of her silky brown hair behind her ear, I feel tiny needle points all over my skin. I wish I could get up the nerve to go sit down next to her at lunch, but then I think, *What if she laughs and walks away?*

I miss California.

* * *

But that afternoon, I do get some good news. True to her word, the vice-principal has gotten me switched to a more advanced math class, one that'll teach me more than to count to ten. The class is in the room right next to my old one, so as soon as the last bell rings Luke and I meet in the hall and head out of school just like before. Unfortunately, as we walk down the steps of Big Sky Middle School, Brad Mullen, Clyde Crookshank, and Harold Dicks appear from behind a pickup truck.

"Well, well," Brad sneers. "Look who's here— California Boy."

Clyde and Harold snicker. Luke and I try to keep walking, but Brad plants himself in front of us.

"We've missed you, California," he says.

That's been no accident. Taking Luke's advice, I've done everything I can to stay off of Brad's game trails the past couple of weeks. I guess it hasn't been enough.

"So where you been?" Brad says, bunching the front of my T-shirt in his fist. "Just because you're in the brainy math class now doesn't mean we can't still be friends."

Tapeworm and Maggot get a big thump out of this joke. I notice that today Brad's breath smells like decaying fish.

"Just around," I tell him, my heart hammering so loud I'm sure he can hear it.

"Around, huh? I think you've been avoiding me, you little chicken gizzard, and I...don't...like...it." He puts his face close to mine, and I can't help noticing his mouthful of brown teeth and bleeding gums. I've already been in Coffee long enough to recognize the signs of a die-hard tobacco-chewer.

"I haven't been avoiding you," I tell him, trying to draw away, but his fist holds me like iron. "I have a different schedule."

Brad looks at Harold and smirks. "A different schedule—like he's a goddamn stockbroker or somethin'." Both of the Parasites laugh and Brad turns back to me. I can tell he's looking for an excuse to clobber me, but not giving it to him is currently Guy's Number One Priority in Life.

"Aw…Brad, ease up," Luke ventures. I admire his courage, but it only feeds Brad's violent creativity.

"I'll ease both of you up my fist," he snarls. "You both make me puke. Especially you, Calf Crap. Think you can just come to my town and do what you want? Why don't you get the hell out of Coffee, anyway?"

Show me the way, I think as Brad shoves me to the ground. He gathers up a good mouthful of tobacco juice and spits, hitting me right in the chest. I'm shaking with adrenaline, but at the same time I'm amazed what a good shot he is. It's too bad spitting isn't an Olympic sport.

"Get the hell out of here," Brad says, his bullying quota temporarily satisfied. "And don't be avoidin' me anymore or I'll come find you."

* * *

Neither Luke nor I say much as we walk back to my house. When we get there I say, "You mind if we skip the math lesson today?"

Luke shrugs. "That's okay. What're you going to do tonight?"

"I don't know. Not much."

"Yeah, me either."

Then I ask something that's been on my mind. "Hey, Luke?"

"Yeah?"

"A couple of weeks ago, Brad said your family almost ruined this town."

I see color rush into Luke's face.

"I don't believe him or anything," I quickly add. "I was just wondering why he's so mad at you. I mean, I see why he's mad at me—being from California and all—but you're one of the nicest people in this town."

Luke tugs on his earlobe. "It's nothing," he says, looking away.

"I'm sorry," I say. "It's none of my business."

And it isn't. After my dad left, my mom, my teachers—and even one of my mom's friends—were always asking how I *felt* about my father leaving or if I wanted to *talk* about it. At first I tried to answer their questions. I tried to tell them I felt like someone had run over my chest with a steamroller. Sometimes I even let myself cry in front of them. Then I realized that no matter how much I talked or what I said, no one really had a clue what I was going through. They just wanted me to talk to make *themselves* feel better.

That doesn't mean I don't want to know what happened to Luke. It's just that I understand that whatever happened, he's had to deal with it on his own. It's his own business if he does or doesn't want to talk about it.

We stand there for another moment. Then I say, "Well, see you tomorrow?"

Luke stares at the ground like he almost wants to tell me something, but instead he nods. "Yeah, okay. See you tomorrow."

* * *

After Luke leaves I drag myself into the house. Streak greets me before I can close the front door. He jumps up, wagging his stump, but not even his wet dog kisses cheer me up this afternoon.

"Guy, that you?" Grandpa hollers from the kitchen. For an old man he's still got an annoyingly powerful set of lungs.

"Yeah, Grandpa."

"Come say howdy, son."

I'm not much in a "howdy" mood, but I drop my pack and walk in with Streak nipping at my shoelaces.

"Do me a favor. Get me some grapes to graze on," Grandpa says as I enter the kitchen.

I take some grapes out of the refrigerator and rinse them off under the faucet, then put them on a plate and hand them to Grandpa.

"Thanks, son. So, how was the old brain factory today?"

I shrug. I've got my head in the refrigerator again, looking for something to drink. There isn't much. We're all out of root beer and I've drunk enough of Mom's cranberry juice to last a lifetime.

"Well, you look like you fell into a hole," Grandpa continues, popping a grape into his mouth. "And in my experience, that usually means girl trouble, bully trouble, or both."

I look at Grandpa, surprised that he'd know such a thing. "It's nothing," I tell him.

"So you're sayin' you been chewin' tobacco and spittin' on your own shirt?"

I'd forgotten about the shirt. Again I shrug and try to hide behind the open refrigerator door.

"Guy, do you think you're the only person who's seen trouble before?" Grandpa asks. "Your friend Luke—his family's been through more barbed wire than any dozen families oughta have to go through with that gold mine business."

I straighten up. "What do you mean? What gold mine?"

Grandpa puts up his hand. "Never mind. That's a story for him to tell you when he's ready. But I can see as plain as winter wheat you've got things on your mind, and sometimes spreadin' the weight around can help. Have a seat and tell me about it."

With a sigh I close the refrigerator door and lean back against the kitchen counter. Up until now, Grandpa's been pretty good about staying out of my business. He's never grilled me about my dad leaving or anything like that, so I decide to cut him some slack. He probably just wants the company.

"Well, there's this girl I like," I begin, "but she's not my big problem."

"Your big problem is Brad Mullen."

I stare at Grandpa and this time, I'm not surprised. I'm shocked. "How did you know that?"

"You forget where you're living, buddy boy. Everyone knows about the Mullens around here. Trouble sticks to them like manure on—what's that stuff they use to fasten clothes?"

I think for a moment. "Velcro."

"Yeah, like manure on Velcro."

"Why is that?"

Grandpa shifts his lower jaw thoughtfully to one side and stares up at the kitchen light. "Can't say for sure. Maybe the Mullens have bad genes. More likely it's money. Money isn't everything, but when you don't have enough for the basics, trouble seems to find you a lot more often. And for one reason or another, the Mullens have been poor a long time."

Grandpa pauses and then says, "Anyhoots, I've still got buddies down at the Union Club. They tell me Brad's got it in for the new kid."

"That's an understatement," I say, finally sitting down at the table. "He's just looking for an excuse to punch my clock."

Grandpa chuckles and I find that a little annoying, considering we could be talking about my departure for the next world.

"That sounds like a Mullen," Grandpa says. "So what's your plan?"

I shake my head. "I don't know. I guess sooner or later I'm going to have to fight him."

"That'd be how a good Western would end—with a big showdown. A good fight—especially a good sacrifice. Yep. That ought to be a real crowd-pleaser."

I don't quite like the tone in Grandpa's voice—and I definitely don't like the word *sacrifice*. "What do you mean?"

Grandpa pops another grape into his mouth. "Now don't get me wrong, son. I think you've got plenty of heart, but let's face it. You fight Brad Mullen and you'll be a punching bag for him. But hey," he adds, "if that's the way you want to play it."

Now I'm really annoyed. "What would *you* do?"

Grandpa chews for a while, then swallows. "Well, I was under the impression you had a pretty good thinking cap under that crazy hair of yours. At least as good as Brad's and probably a good sight better."

"I get by," I tell him.

"So why are you letting Brad Mullen pick the field of battle?"

I look at my grandfather and then down at Streak. Grandpa, I realize, is a lot smarter than I ever gave him credit for.

"You have any ideas?" I ask.

"Naw. This is your show and I'm confident you can handle it. Just remember one thing: The best victory is one where the other guy wins, too."

Chapter Seven

The following day in English, Mrs. Minneman hands out our next assignment, a book called *Animal Farm*. "Great," I whisper to Luke. "A book about farming."

Luke stifles a laugh. "It's not about farming. Haven't you ever heard of George Orwell?"

The name sounds familiar. "Didn't he used to coach the Washington Redskins?" I ask.

This time Luke's laugh erupts before he can stuff it. Several kids turn around to look at us—including Catherine. My heart freezes, then fires off like an M-80. Catherine smiles at me through her red-rimmed glasses, but before I can figure out what kind of smile it is, she turns around and Mrs. Minneman starts her morning lecture.

"Now that you've gotten warmed up with *The Watsons Go to Birmingham,*" she tells us, "it's time to sink your teeth into something even pithier."

I'm not sure what "pithier" means, but it can't be good.

"The Watsons Go to Birmingham," Mrs. Minneman explains, "deals with the topic of racism—the oppression of one group of people by another, specifically black people by whites. *Animal Farm* also deals with oppression, but examines it in a more general context as part of human nature."

"Sounds like big fun," I mutter.

"For tonight's homework, I want you to read the first two chapters. We'll talk about them tomorrow."

I sigh. But then I look again at Catherine, who's busy counting Mrs. Minneman's syllables on her fingertips. I think, *Maybe I'd have something to say to Catherine if I read the assignment for a change.*

That sounds so lame—doing your homework so some girl might take a look at you—but I'm tired of waiting around for things to happen to me. In California, I *did* things. I skateboarded, learned to surf, played video games with my friends. But here, my only friend is Luke and he's not into skateboarding or any of the stuff I used to do. I guess I could try to make other friends, but so far all most kids seem to talk about around here is cars and hunting and fishing—stuff I couldn't care less about. Besides, I think word's gotten out that I'm on Brad's hit list. Whenever I walk by a group of guys, they stop talking or tense up like I've got swine flu or something. Maybe they think that if they're friends with me, Brad will sight in on them, too.

I don't know what the answer is. I just know I'm tired of feeling like I'm in a foreign country where everyone knows the rules but me.

* * *

At least Sasquatch isn't waiting for me after school. Luke and I both breathe sighs of relief as we head down the steps of Big Sky and see nothing but smooth sailing back to my house. As we start walking, I think about what Grandpa told me about Luke's family. I feel like asking Luke more about it, but he starts chattering away happily about something that happened in his P.E. class this afternoon, and I don't want to bring him down by prying into his past. And again, his skeletons are none of my business unless he decides to tell me about them. So as Luke launches into a new story about a girl and her horse, I turn my mind toward getting Brad off my case.

Grandpa's right, I think. *Outsmarting Brad is definitely the way to go. It's the only way to go if I want to stay out of the hospital.*

I consider different ideas to get him off my back. They range from digging a bully trap for him outside his front door to trying to get him to like me by acting as mean as he is. *Maybe I could buy him an ice cream or pack of chewing tobacco,* I think, but that sounds even stupider than my other ideas.

"Hey, there's Streak!" Luke says as we approach my house.

"Huh?" I say, following Luke's finger. Behind the new-and-improved gate, Streak sits patiently watching our approach.

"How's the dog?" Luke asks in his best doggy voice. As Luke opens the gate, Streak leaps into the air and gives him a big lick. Then Streak gives my cheek a slurp.

"Hey, good boy!" I say, kneeling down so Streak can wriggle in and out of my arms. I love this dog. He cheers me up just by being himself.

"Here ya go," Luke says, picking up the tennis ball, which by now looks and smells like it's been floating in a septic tank. Luke chucks it toward the back of the yard and Streak tears after it.

"He's the fastest dog I ever saw," Luke says.

"Yeah, he's pretty fast." I try to sound modest.

"Aw...that reminds me," Luke says. "Did you hear about the Fall Fair?"

"I heard the announcement at school." Before Mrs. Minneman's class this morning, Principal Goode came on the intercom and announced that the Fall Fair would be held the weekend after next. I'd never heard of a Fall Fair, but quickly learned it was some kind of fundraiser to help pay for the rest of the year's activities.

"Aw...I was thinking Streak would be perfect for it."

"Perfect for what?" I ask.

"The Frisbee contest."

Luke takes the ball from Streak and tosses it again. I have no idea what he's talking about, but the word "Frisbee" gets my attention. Back in California my friends and I used to play Ultimate Frisbee all the time.

"You know," Luke tells me again. "*The Frisbee contest.* Every year at the Fall Fair, there's a dog Frisbee-catching contest. You bring your dog and see how many times he can catch the Frisbee in a minute. They score you by how far you throw the Frisbee and whether your dog leaps into the air to catch it. Streak would be perfect for that."

"There's only one problem," I tell Luke. "Streak can't catch a Frisbee."

"Do you have one?"

"Yeah, I think so."

I go into the house, say a quick hi to Grandpa—just long enough to pour him a glass of V8—and rummage through the boxes in the back of my closet. After a few minutes, I unearth a beat-up Frisbee I brought from California.

"Aw...perfect," Luke says when I return to the backyard. "Let's see what ole Streak can do."

Streak drops his ball and eyes the Frisbee curiously as Luke pulls his arm back. Luke gives a couple of fake throws to let Streak know that it's a game. Then he flings the faded blue disc across the backyard. It's not a good throw and dives quickly, but Streak bounds after it. He doesn't try to catch it, instead waiting until it hits the ground before snatching it up. He does carry it back to us, though—a good sign.

"Here, let me try," I say. I make a short side-armed throw with the disc, causing it to float longer than Luke's throw. Streak is waiting for it when it comes down and it bonks him on the head. Luke and I laugh, but Streak enthusiastically grabs the disc and rushes back to us.

Luke and I begin trading off throwing the Frisbee.

On the third throw, Streak snaps at the Frisbee as it comes down.

On the fourth and fifth throws, he looks like he's trying to catch it.

On the sixth throw, he actually seizes it in his mouth and Luke and I whoop for joy.

By the tenth throw, Streak is leaping into the air to intercept the Frisbee when it's still three or four feet off the ground.

I try to give Streak a doggie treat as a reward, but he shakes me off. He just wants another chance at that Frisbee.

"He's a natural," Luke says as I toss the disc again.

"He really is," I agree, still not quite believing it. "I don't know why I never tried this before. Do you think he'll be good enough to compete in the Fall Fair?"

Luke laughs. "He's *already* good enough for the fair. He might even win."

"How many people usually compete?"

"Maybe ten, fifteen. But only a couple of the dogs will give Streak a run for it."

"Who won last year?" I take the Frisbee from Streak and stop to look at Luke, who has become strangely silent.

"Well?" I ask him.

"Brad Mullen and his dog Shep."

* * *

After Luke leaves, I chat with Grandpa for a few minutes and then head to my room. Streak follows me and lies down as I pick out a CD and put it in the changer. My stereo's old, but it still works fine. Over the last few years I've managed to scrape together a pretty good CD collection. Mom keeps trying to push folk and classical music on me, but most of my stuff is harder rock—Led Zeppelin, Guns N' Roses, the Rolling Stones, Pink Floyd, and Neil Young and Crazy Horse. A lot of my CDs were my dad's, but I've also got some newer bands like Social Distortion and Green Day and Jim's Big Ego.

I hit the Play button, put on my headphones, and flop down on my bed. A moment later, the first beats of Pink Floyd's *The Wall* fill my brain. The opening notes lift my body off the mattress and I close my eyes and float with the music.

I can't always listen to my dad's CDs. Sometimes they make me miss him too much or get angry at him for leaving. Other times, though, they put me into a comfortable place to think about stuff and what's going on. This is one of those times. I wonder again what Catherine's smile meant earlier in English class and what she's doing right now. I think about my reading assignment for the night—and kick it back out of my head. Then I glance down at Streak and marvel at how fast he learned to catch the Frisbee. I haven't made up my mind about entering him in the Fall Fair. I love the idea of kicking Brad's butt in the contest, but I don't have to think much further to realize I'd be the one to get the final butt-kickin' if Streak and I did manage to pull it off.

Eventually I tune out thoughts about the contest and sink deeper into the music. I'm almost completely zoned when I hear a loud knock on my bedroom door. I open my eyes and tug the headphones off.

"Yeah?" I say.

My mom opens the door.

"Oh, hi," I say, still pulling my brain out of "The Wall."

"Hi," she says. "The power company just called to report an unusual drain on their electricity supply. I thought it might be from your stereo."

"Hey, I'm using my headphones. How did you know I was listening to music?"

"It was too quiet. I figured you were in here assaulting your tympanic nerves."

"Don't worry, I don't have it up too high."

Mom smiles. "I'm glad to hear it. I don't want you needing a hearing aid like Grandpa."

"How was work?" I ask.

Mom sits down on the edge of my bed and lets out a sigh. She looks beat. "Helping people pick out wallpaper isn't quite the career move I always dreamed it would be."

I snort and ask, "Does that mean we can move back to California?"

"No," my mom says, trying to hide her annoyance. "This is our home—for now, at least. Besides, I'll figure out something better. Hey, how's school going?"

I shrug. "It's okay."

"You're not having any problems with the kids or anything?"

"Just the usual," I lie. "It's no big deal."

Once or twice I've debated whether to tell her about Brad Mullen, but I figure she's got enough to worry about. Also, she's pretty clueless about this kind of stuff. Maybe because of her training as a behavioral therapist, she always believes that just below the surface of any creep is some angel waiting to come out. She doesn't get it that some people act creepy because they *are* creepy.

"How are your classes?" Mom asks.

"Mostly pretty good," I say.

"English?"

"Yeah, well..."

I expect her to chastise me or give me a pep talk, but instead, she says, "You know, when I was your age, I hated English, too."

My eyes widen. "You did?" The way books are always welded to her hand, it's the last thing I expect her to say.

She nods and tucks a strand of her hair behind her ear—a lot like Catherine does, I realize.

"Yep. I remember I had this teacher, Mrs. Bartoletti. She was a great teacher, but I didn't know it at the time. She'd start reading poetry and her eyes would go all misty. She seemed to know every poem by heart and would just let the book fall by her side as the poems poured out of her. After school, my friends and I would make fun of her, inventing our own silly rhymes and pretending to cry."

"So what changed your mind about books?" I ask.

She ponders this for a moment.

"Believe it or not, I think it was your father," she finally says, turning her blue eyes toward me.

"But you always said he had a math brain."

"He did—does," she says, shifting her gaze back out the window. "But when I first met him in college, he always carried a book around with him. Books about philosophy and politics and history. He seemed to want to absorb everything all at once. I wasn't really interested in the books myself. I think I started reading to impress him, but eventually I got hooked."

Mom gets really far away for a moment, then snaps her eyes back toward me and puts her hand on my leg. "Anyway, Guy, I know you don't like English, but I hope you put some effort into it. I want you to have more options than your grandparents did. Or than other kids around here will have without a good education."

* * *

After Mom leaves to fix dinner, I think about what she said. "What the hell," I mutter. I turn off my stereo and dig out *Animal Farm* from my backpack. Lying back down on my bed, I open the book. I skip the introduction—just the word "Introduction" makes me feel like falling into a coma—and plunge into chapter one.

It's slow going. I don't know much about plot, but I know I like action and this book begins about as fast as a poisoned slug. After a couple of pages, though, I realize that the book definitely isn't about farming, and that's a relief. It's about these animals that get ticked off at people and take over the farm where they live. In between taking breaks to throw the Frisbee for Streak and eating dinner and catching *The Simpsons* on television, I manage to finish chapters one and two. I don't *like* doing it, but I do it. I think it's the first time I've ever finished an English assignment on time, and I'm so proud of myself that I go ahead and read chapter three, too.

Chapter Eight

The next day, I take my seat in English and Principal Goode blesses our day over the PA system. Mrs. Minneman gets up from her desk and asks, "So, how does everyone like *Animal Farm* so far?"

Nobody says anything for a moment. Then a kid named Dylan raises his hand and says, "It's kind of boring."

Right on, Dylan, I think.

Then a girl raises her hand and says, "It's not that it's boring, exactly. It's, like, weird."

Mrs. Minneman laughs. "Okay. I can see how those are valid criticisms. But what is it about? You've got these farm animals and they force the people off the farm and start running it for themselves. What is going on?"

After a moment, Catherine raises her hand. I'm always glad when she does this because it gives me a good excuse to watch her without seeming too obvious.

"The book isn't about animals," she says. "It's about people."

"Go on," says Mrs. Minneman.

"Well, I think all the different animals represent different kinds of people in society. Some are better at some things than others are and some seem smarter."

Before I know what I'm doing, I also raise my hand and say, "Yeah, the pigs all know how to read and write. But Boxer can only learn the first four letters of the alphabet."

Silence drops over the classroom. Luke and the other kids just stare at me and I can feel my face turn into a tomato. I don't know what I said wrong, but I'm sure I should have kept my mouth shut.

Finally Mrs. Minneman speaks. "You're absolutely right, Guy. But I think you've been reading ahead."

I suddenly realize that the part I just talked about was from chapter three, and we were only supposed to read through chapter two. "Oh, right," I mutter. "Sorry."

Instead of being upset, Mrs. Minneman gets this goofy look on her face like she's pleased. We go on to talk about other aspects of the book and what they might mean. I don't raise my hand again, but I can pretty much follow everything that's being said. By the end of class, I feel something I've never felt in English before—average.

It feels kind of good.

* * *

Later that day during Spanish, I receive a note to come to the counselor's office. There are only twenty minutes left in the period, so I gather up my books and head down there, wondering what's going on. I'm almost positive it's about my D on the English paper, but at the same time it seems a bit early in the semester to be dragging me out of class for a pep talk.

The counselor's office is tucked in with the administrative offices. I hand the note to the school secretary, Mrs. Bellweather. She glances at it and says, "Go on in."

As I enter, I see the counselor, Mr. Doolebaum, reading some papers at his desk. I've seen him around before. He's hard to miss. He towers over everyone else, and he strides through the halls with a permanent smile stretching his lips. Everyone calls him Mr. D. He's always wearing these funky shirts with a turquoise and silver bolo tie. Even more shocking, he has a long black ponytail—the only one I've seen on a man since moving to Montana.

When he sees me, he leaps to his feet and exclaims, "Guy! Come on in." He's about the first person I've met here who doesn't try to shake my hand, and that scores him some points.

"Pull up a seat," he says, closing the door behind me. I cautiously sit down.

He sits in a chair opposite me and somehow manages to cross his long legs into what looks like a stable, if not exactly comfortable, position.

"Welcome to Big Sky," he begins. "I'm Mr. Doolebaum."

"I know."

He chuckles to himself. "I suppose you do. I kind of stick out around here, don't I? I hope I didn't scare you by calling you into the office like this, but you've been here over a month now, and I like to sit down and meet with all of the students near the beginning of the year—especially the new kids."

I nod, but don't say anything.

"So, you're from California. How are you liking Montana so far?" he asks.

"It's got its high points."

This time he laughs out loud. "And its low ones, too, I'll bet. You know, I'm not from around here either. I moved out from New York about twenty years ago. I came to Montana for the mountains and wilderness, and I got along fine with them. The people took more time. Man," he said, grasping his ponytail, "you should have seen the way people looked at me with *this*. Eventually, though, we all got used to each other."

I smile politely, wondering where exactly this male bonding is supposed to be heading.

"How are your classes? You like them okay? Any problem spots?"

"They're fine," I tell him. "I probably need to work harder in English."

He gives a small wave of his hand. "Yeah, well, we've all got one of those. What about the kids? You doing alright with them?" he asks me.

"They're okay," I say. "Most of them."

Another laugh. Then Mr. D grows more serious. "You might not think it, but kids around here face the same issues they do in California. Drugs. Alcoholic parents. Bullying."

Aha, I think. *So that's it. The main topic of the day is Brad Mullen.*

But then Mr. D catches me off guard.

"Divorce is one of the biggest things kids have to go through," he continues. "Right here in Coffee, almost half of all children have experienced divorce in their families."

Immediately my defenses go on alert, and I realize this conversation may not be about bullying after all.

Mr. D uncrosses his legs and looks over at a folder on his desk. "It says here your own folks are divorced."

I groan inside. I can't believe he's brought this up.

"I don't know," I tell him.

This seems to confuse him. "You mean, they're still together?"

"No, but I don't know if they're divorced or not."

"Oh yeah, right." Mr. D shifts a little and again tries a sideways approach. "My own parents split up when I was about your age," he tells me. "It was one of the hardest things I ever had to go through."

"Uh-huh."

Mr. D doesn't know it yet, but battle lines have just been drawn. I've been through this kind of conversation a dozen times before, and he's no match for me. As he talks, I quickly close the iron gates to my castle. My archers move into position and my catapults are loaded. In case all that fails, the burning oil is poised, just waiting to pour down on anyone trying to scale the walls.

Mr. D, though, marches forward, probably thinking

he's launching the cleverest assault in the history of counselor-student relationships.

"I was really mad at my folks for a long time," he tells me. "Really angry, you know?"

In my mind, I catch a brief glimpse of myself in our kitchen the year before in California. My mom is standing nearby and I'm screaming at her. "Why? Why did he leave? What did you *do* to him?"

But my lips stay pressed together. To Mr. Doolebaum, I just nod and mutter, "Mmm-hmmm."

"Even now," he continues, "I sometimes wonder if I ever really got over the whole thing." Mr. D pauses. "Do you ever feel angry at your parents, Guy?"

Something tries to climb up out of me, but I stab it back down with my sword. "Nope," I tell him.

"Do you ever blame yourself for what happened? A lot of kids do. I think that I did."

My castle walls start to tremble as I remember the weeks after my father left. I walked from room to room in our house, looking for clues to why he had gone, wondering if I had done something wrong to force him away. But I steady myself and order the catapults to fire.

"No," I tell Mr. Doolebaum. "I've never thought that."

"Oh. Well, many kids do, and it isn't their fault. It's usually the adults who create the problem and, unfortunately, the kids get caught in the crossfire."

I don't react.

Mr. Doolebaum looks at me and falls silent for a moment. I think he is finally realizing that his invading hordes have met their match. He forces another smile.

"Well," he says. "It would be understandable if you did...feel like that. And if you ever want to talk about it or anything else, I hope you feel free to just drop by."

The bell rings, signaling the end of the period.

"Remember, Guy. It doesn't matter what it is—difficulty with classes, Brad Mullen, whatever. Just know I'm here for you."

I nod and quickly stand up. As I exit the office, though, I suddenly feel a little wobbly and reach my hand out to a nearby counter. Nobody seems to notice and the moment passes. Taking a deep breath, I head off to my next class.

* * *

The following Monday, Brad Mullen gets caught trying to shove a sixth-grader into the cafeteria dishwasher and earns four solid days of morning and afternoon detention. This is undoubtedly a real drag for the sixth-grader, but for Luke and me, it's like winning the lottery. Our prize is four glorious days without having to look over our shoulders and we decide to make the most of it. After school every day, we head straight to my house. We practice throwing the Frisbee for Streak and I've got to admit Luke is right. Streak is a natural and soon catches the Frisbee like he's been doing it his whole life.

After the second day, Grandpa even comes out to

watch. While we throw, Grandpa eats grapes and reminisces about dogs he used to have. It seems like he's had four or five thousand of them, all with names like T-Bone and Lollipop and Moonshine, but Luke and I don't mind hearing about them. Grandpa looks especially happy watching Streak chase after the Frisbee, and I realize he must have been pretty lonely living in this house since Grandma died.

When we're done working with Streak on the Frisbee, we go inside to do our math homework together. I whip through advanced algebra and geometry from my new class and then attempt to guide Luke through his basic algebra and geometry problems. As usual, it's slow going and I lose my patience more than once.

"Luke," I shout at him one afternoon, "x-squared is not the same thing as two times x!"

"Oh, right. I forgot. It's just that when x equals two, it ends up being the same thing."

"Uhhhh," I moan, letting my head roll back on my shoulders.

Fortunately, Luke doesn't seem to mind when I act like a jerk. After that, whenever I get ready to blow my lid, I call out "Frisbee break!" and we play with Streak for a while.

When Luke goes home, I put on my headphones and daydream about Catherine for a while. Then, I dive back into *Animal Farm*. By chapter five, I can see where the book is going. The animals have kicked the people off the farm, but now the pigs are turning into the masters, just like the people were. It's a strange book and isn't nearly as fun as playing a video game, but something besides passing English keeps me reading. It's not really like anything else I've read. Once or twice, I even find myself thinking about it as I walk to school and talking about it with Luke while we're playing Frisbee.

I wonder if my dad ever read it?

* * *

Unfortunately, Brad's four days of detention end far too quickly. On the Friday before the Fall Fair, I find myself in a familiar position—shoved up against the school wall with Brad breathing toxic fumes into my face.

"Where've you been, Chicken Gizzard?" he demands.

My instinct is to grovel as usual, but I've been anticipating this moment all week and am ready to try something different.

"Hey, Brad," I say. "I hear you've got a Frisbee dog."

I feel his grip on my collar loosen. "Yeah, what about it?"

"Well, uh, I hear he's pretty good."

Brad presses me against the wall again. "Shep's not pretty good. He's the best."

"Are you competing tomorrow?"

"Damn right I am. And I'm going to *win!* What do you care, Scrotum Head?"

I pause long enough to appreciate Brad's latest name for me—and give myself one last chance to back out—but decide to go for it. "Well," I tell him, "I'm entering my dog in the contest, too."

Brad doesn't know how to react to this information, and I figure it can go two ways. It can either tick him off so much that he pounds me into fungus food right then and there, or he can see the contest as another opportunity to humiliate me, which is what I'm counting on.

Luckily, Brad goes for Option B. His mouth spreads into an ugly sneer and he looks back at Clyde and Harold. "Did you hear that? This butt wipe thinks he can beat me and Shep in the Frisbee contest!"

The Parasites guffaw like village idiots as the morning bell goes off. Brad lets go of me and says, "See you tomorrow, loser."

* * *

A few minutes later, in English class, Mrs. Minneman hands out our assignment. We've finished reading *Animal Farm* and have to write a paper on it. I figured it was coming, but now I groan along with a couple of the other English-challenged kids.

"The first draft of your paper is due next Friday," Mrs. Minneman explains, "and I'm going to give you a lot of leeway on what to write. Maybe you want to compare the book to real events in the world. Perhaps you'd like to compare the story to other works of literature. Some of you may want to analyze one of the main characters and his role in the book. I'm going to leave this up to you, but feel free to come discuss ideas with me."

"*That's* a big help," I grumble to Luke. "What am I going to write about?"

"I know what I'm going to write about," says Luke. "I'm going to compare *Animal Farm* to what happened in the former Soviet Union."

Sometimes I can't believe this kid. "How'd you come up with *that?*"

Luke shrugs. "Aw...I don't know. I just thought of it. It's not that original."

It is to me. I have to admit that sometimes I still think of Luke as pretty simple, but he keeps coming up with these surprising ideas. I look over at Catherine and wonder what she's going to write about. It'll probably be something brilliant, too.

Chapter Nine

The Saturday of the Fall Fair, Luke arrives at my house around nine. Grandpa's still in bed, but my mom has finished her morning reading-and-coffee ritual and is getting ready for work.

"Hi, Luke," my mother says, running some water over last night's dishes in the sink. "You all set for the Fall Fair?"

"Yes, Mrs. Martinez. Streak is going to do great."

Mom laughs. "I'm sure he will, the way you two have been working him. I'm sorry I won't be able to come watch today. Since I'm the new girl in town, I get the weekend shift down at the shop."

"We'll bring you back the blue ribbon," Luke says with a smile. I can tell he believes it.

As we go out to get Streak, I secretly admit that I'm glad my mom has to work. I'm nervous enough as it is, and not just about Brad. I'm sure most of the other kids will be there, including Catherine. I don't want to make a fool out of myself.

* * *

Luke and I arrive at Big Sky about ten o'clock and the schoolyards are already hoppin'. The Fall Fair is a much bigger deal than I expected. A lot of tables are hocking homemade baked goods, crafts, pencils, T-shirts with school logos—anything that can make a buck. Raffle tickets are being sold for everything from backpacks to movie passes to a trip to Spokane, and vendors are peddling hot dogs, cotton candy, and soft drinks.

Streak strains at his leash, pulling me toward a stand where a man is making some sort of strange-looking sandwich with something that looks like pita bread. Several people eagerly stand in line, their money ready.

"What are those?" I ask Luke.

"Haven't you ever had Indian Tacos?" he asks.

"I didn't know Indians *made* tacos," I say. "I thought tacos came from Mexico."

"Not these."

"What are they made of?"

"I don't know exactly. Fried bread stuffed with beans and a lot of spicy stuff. They're good—but you'd better wait till after the contest to eat one."

"Why?"

"Aw...they can sit kind of heavy in your gut. Once I ate one and—"

I hold up my hand. "Luke, I don't want to hear about it."

Country music blares as we take a quick cruise of the booths and exhibits—or, rather, Streak takes *us* on a quick cruise. Before long, his quivering nose leads us to a fenced-off area full of sheep, goats, and cows.

"Hey, what are these doing here?" I ask.

"Why wouldn't they be here? It's a fair," Luke says.

When comprehension still fails to register on my face, he continues, "A lot of kids around here raise animals. The judges give out awards for the best ones."

I shake my head. "I never saw sheep and cows at my school in California."

"In case you forgot, you're in Montana now."

As Streak sniffs a cage full of strange-looking rabbits with especially long ears, the familiar voice of Principal Goode cuts into the sound system. He welcomes everybody to the Fall Fair and urges us to spend as much money as possible. Then he announces the first of the day's events—the three-legged race.

"Aw...you want to do that?" Luke asks.

I shake my head. "No way. I'll go watch, though."

We walk over to the starting line for the three-legged race. A crowd has already gathered and I glance around for Brad Mullen and the Parasites. Instead, we run into Catherine.

"Hello, Guy," she says. "Hi, Luke."

I've never heard Catherine say my name before and it kind of throws me.

"Hi, Catherine," Luke says.

"Oh, uh, hi," I mumble, my tongue feeling like a beached whale. "Is this your dog?" Catherine asks, kneeling down.

I'm about to tell her that Streak isn't much of a petting dog, but he steps right up to her and lets her rub his chest and ears.

Luke answers for me. "Yep. That's Streak."

"Oh, *goood* boy," Catherine croons. "What is he, Border collie and what else?"

I'm amazed at how much everyone seems to know about animals around here. "Uh, I'm not sure. He's kind of a mutt."

"I think he's got some Australian cattle dog in him," Luke says.

"Oh, I can see that now," Catherine says. "Oooh, what a good dog. Are you entering him in the Frisbee contest?"

"Yeah," I say. "Luke and I have been practicing."

"Practicing *what?*" Brad Mullen barges between us. His big German shepherd jumps all over Streak. I start to reach for my dog, but he knows what to do. He rolls over in a submissive posture and then, his ears laid back, begins to lick Brad's dog on the face.

Brad sneers. "Butt-wipe owner, butt-wipe dog, huh?"

Clyde Crookshank and Harold Dicks snort behind him.

I feel myself turning red and am looking for a way to slink off, but Catherine stands up and brushes off the knees of her pants. "Brad," she says, "don't you ever get tired of trying to prove how much testosterone you have?"

Brad hesitates for a moment. Then he blusters, "At least I have more than you do."

Luke, Catherine, and I crack up. "Thank goodness for that," Catherine says.

Now it's Brad's turn to blush. To top it off, Streak stands up and walks behind Brad. Before I can stop him, he shoves his nose forward and gives Brad a massive butt sniff.

Brad yelps and spins around, kicking wildly, but Streak is way too quick. He dodges around Brad, tangling him up in his leash. Again I try to grab Streak, but it's too late. Brad takes one step and crashes into the grass.

All around us, people burst into laughter—even the Parasites. Shep lets out a playful bark and dives into the fray, licking Brad on the face.

"Get away, dammit!" Brad swears, trying to shove Shep away while still kicking at Streak. I untangle them and pull off my dog.

"I've got to go," says Catherine, still grinning. "Good luck, you two. I'm sure Streak will do great."

She walks off, leaving my heart slam dancing inside my chest. Brad leaps up, ready to spit nails. Unfortunately, I know that it's my hide the nails are going to fly into. He reaches forward to grab me, but spots Principal Goode glaring at him. Shaking with rage, he pretends to flick something off of my shirt and says under his breath, "You are dead meat, California. First my dog is going to kick your dog's ass. Then I'm going to kick yours."

He spits a big glop of tobacco juice at the ground and snarls, "Have a nice day."

"Whew," I sigh as Brad drags his German shepherd away. "Is Fall Fair always this much fun?"

"Aw...we've had it, Guy," Luke says. "Brad's going to kill us both."

Luke isn't usually so pessimistic, but I have no doubt he's right. "I know, but seeing him crash into the lawn was worth anything else that happens today."

"You think maybe we should just skip the Frisbee contest?"

I admit I'm thinking the same thing. I must have been temporarily insane deciding to go up against Brad in the contest, and now with Streak's butt-sniff move, I'm pretty much doomed. On the other hand, it also means I've got nothing to lose. If we enter the contest, Brad's going to beat me to a pulp, win or lose. If we don't enter, he's still going to beat me to a pulp.

Nearby, a P.E. teacher shouts, "Go!" and the first round of contestants in the three-legged race starts bounding toward the finish line. Luke ignores them. "The problem is that Streak really needs this experience if he's going to do well in the city meet."

"What are you talking about? What city meet?"

The crowd is screaming encouragement to the three-legged racers and Luke has to shout for me to hear him. "I told you about the city meet!"

"No, you didn't! What is it?"

"The City Frisbee Dog Championship. It's sponsored by Gulp Pet Foods Company. It's a national thing. If Streak wins there, he can go on to the regional competition in Missoula the following weekend. If he finishes in the top two there, he qualifies for State."

"You didn't say anything about that!"

"Maybe I thought you knew."

"How would I know that?" I ask him, exasperated.

As the cheering dies down, Luke asks, "Well, are you going to enter Streak or should we go home?"

After a pause, I bend down to rub Streak's chest. I tell Luke, "Streak is definitely going to catch some Frisbees today."

Chapter Ten

The Frisbee-throwing contest is scheduled for noon—*high noon*, I think—and there are a lot more entrants than Luke had predicted. I count at least twenty other students with their dogs gathered around the throwing area. Almost everyone else at the fair has gathered near the football field, and there's no question this is going to be the day's most popular event.

"Terrific," I mutter, feeling the pressure crank up a couple of hundred atmospheres. Streak paces excitedly, straining on his leash to say hello to every person around him and sniff every mongrel in sight. I scan the crowd, hoping for a glimpse of Catherine.

"Isn't this great?" Luke says, stopping to pet a little dog that looks like a rug with legs. He informs me it's called a corgi and then starts rattling off trivia about every other breed around us. They range from smaller poodles and terriers to big dogs like Labs and German shepherds. I have a hard time absorbing what Luke is telling me. I just keep glancing over at Brad and Shep, my stomach twisting tighter than a tourniquet.

Principal Goode makes his way through the crowd and holds up a portable megaphone, which gives off a deafening squeal the first time he talks into it. Half the people shove fingers into their ears. Streak lets out a loud howl, and several other dogs join in. Principal Goode turns down the volume and tries again.

"Welcome, everyone. All the contestants for the Frisbee competition, please gather around while I explain the rules." A couple more kid-dog teams make their way to my vicinity and we listen above the chatter of the crowd.

Principal Goode reels off the rules and they're pretty simple. From the throwing spot, there are four lines, 10, 20, 30, and 40 yards away. Dogs earn 1, 2, 3, or 5 points, depending on which line they clear, plus a half-point bonus if they leap into the air to make the catch. Each of us has a minute to throw the Frisbee. The more successful catches we complete, the higher the score. If two dogs tie, there will be a "throw-off" at the end of the competition.

Each team draws a number to determine the position it will compete in. Of course Streak and I end up with the highest number, which means we're going dead last. As the crowd clears away to give the dogs and throwers room, I feel every blood vessel in my body throb and I breathe in and out like a steam engine.

"Aw...relax, Guy," Luke tells me. "When it's your

turn, just throw it like we've been practicing it and Streak'll do the rest."

"Any other advice?" I ask him.

"Yeah. Don't even worry about the 40-yard mark. Nobody throws it that far. Last year a few people tried because that's worth 5 points. But when they threw too hard, the Frisbee veered off and they didn't get anything. Also, longer throws take more time, so you won't get as many in. Just throw shorter, like we've been doing, and you'll score a lot higher."

"Okay," I say, noticing that Luke is tugging on his earlobe, stretching it out like Play-Doh.

Principal Goode announces the first team, a poodle that belongs to some seventh-grade girl I don't recognize. I figure the dog doesn't have a chance, but it does pretty well. The girl keeps lobbing the Frisbee out there and the poodle runs them down. He catches most of them with his feet on the ground, though, and misses one entirely. Also, the girl doesn't throw the Frisbee farther than 15 or 20 yards, so she and her dog end up scoring only 5 points on four catches.

Next is an Irish setter owned by an eighth-grade boy in my social studies class named Norbert van der Wolf. When Principal Goode yells, "Go!" Norbert flings the Frisbee beyond the 30-yard line and, running hard, the setter snags it. The problem is that as soon as the dog makes the catch, she races off into the crowd. When Norbert finally chases her down, the whistle has already blown.

The dogs and their owners keep competing one by

one. Just before Brad and Shep's turn, a sixth-grade boy and his ugly-looking mutt run onto the field.

"That's a blue heeler," Luke tells me. "See, he's got that compact body and mottled-looking fur."

Whatever he is, man, can that dog jump. When the boy throws the Frisbee, the dog tears after it and just goes airborne, earning bonus points right and left.

"I bet he's five feet off the ground," Luke says with a whistle.

"Parker Boyd," the principal announces when the round is over. "Now in the lead with 11.5 points."

My mood grows bleak. As Grandpa would say, against these dogs Streak and I have about as much chance as a fly in a frog farm. Then Brad is up. He puffs out his chest like he always does, but he moves jerkily and his eyes dart quickly from place to place. That surprises me. I didn't think bullies like Brad got nervous. Before he begins, he bends down and whispers something to Shep that I can't hear—probably something like "You'd better win or I'm going to kick your ass."

Then, Principal Goode shouts, "Ready... Set... Go!"

Brad flings the Frisbee, easily clearing the 30-yard line. Shep's a big dog—more than twice Streak's size—but he moves amazingly fast. He bounds after the disc and leaps into the air after it. An easy 3.5 points.

Shep brings back the Frisbee and Brad rips it out of his mouth and throws again. Shep nabs the next throw for another 3.5 points, but then he misses one altogether. Brad curses and yells, "Shep, get back here!" The dog picks up the fallen disc and bounds back. Brad grabs it out of his mouth and tosses it again, but the miss must have rattled him. Instead of sailing straight, the Frisbee curves left and short. Shep makes the adjustment and dashes after it for two more points.

"Ten seconds to go!" Principal Goode yells and Brad's face scrunches up like a prune. He winds up for the throw and sails a mammoth toss beyond the 40-yard mark. The crowd hushes as Shep races after the Frisbee. It's a long throw, and I'm not sure Shep is going to reach it. With a last dive, though, he catches it just before it hits the ground. He loses the half a bonus point, but the crowd bursts into applause. With 14 points, Brad and Shep have just blasted into the lead.

Brad struts by me with Shep. "Beat that, Calf Crap," he boasts.

After Brad is out of hearing distance, I look at Luke. "I thought no one reached the 40-yard line."

"Aw...well, maybe every once in a while. But it's no problem, Guy. Fifteen points will do it. That's only five good throws. They don't even all have to reach the 30-yard line."

"I don't know, Luke," I say. "I think this is harder than it looks. What if Streak just heads off into the crowd like that Irish setter?"

"He won't."

I don't share his confidence. By the time it's our turn, twenty other dogs have competed. Brad is still in first place, but all eyes focus on Streak and me.

"Competing last today," Principal Goode yells, "are Guy Martinez and his dog, Steak."

The crowd erupts into laughter. "It's *Streak,* not Steak," I tell the principal.

"Oops!" Principal Goode says to more laughter. "Guy Martinez and his dog *Streak.* Are you both ready?"

The answer is no. I'll never be ready for this, but I nod at the starter anyway and whisper to Streak, "Just do your best, buddy."

Out of the corner of my eye I notice Brad and Shep watching from the front of the crowd, but I force them from my mind. I unclip Streak's leash and he darts out a few feet and starts sniffing the ground, probably for the scents of other dogs. I give my special two-note whistle, though, and he snaps his brown eyes back to me, waiting for the first throw.

Principal Goode yells, "Ready... Set... *Go!"*

I pull my arm back and heave the Frisbee way too hard. Streak darts after it, but it veers right and hits the ground before he can get within ten feet of it. My heart sinks as he picks it up and gallops back to me.

"Just relax," Luke shouts, but I'm already sure I've blown it. And if my first throw doesn't seal it, the second one definitely does.

Overcompensating for the first throw, I throw the second one way too soft. Streak is already out to the 30-yard line before he realizes that the Frisbee has barely cleared the 10. He whips around and races back toward it, but he's got no chance. The disc hits the turf before he even comes close.

"So much for the contest," I tell myself.

But then a surprising thing happens. With the pressure off, I relax and throw the next one perfectly. It sails beyond the 30-yard line with just enough "float" in it for Streak to leap up and nab it.

Finally we're on the board, I think.

My fourth throw is like the third and Streak seizes it at least four feet off the ground.

"Fifteen seconds!" Principal Goode yells.

My heart picks up speed and I throw the Frisbee again. It's not the best throw. The disc angles to the right so it's a bit short, but Streak easily adjusts and snags it midair. As he comes racing back to me with the Frisbee in his mouth, we have 9.5 points—and, remarkably, enough time for a sixth throw.

When Principal Goode yells "Five seconds!" I suddenly realize that if I go for a long one, I could actually *beat* Brad.

"Go, Guy!" I hear Luke yell. Other students take up the chant.

I pull my arm back, adrenaline slamming through me, and I heave it as hard as I can.

"Oh no!" I gasp. Because I've thrown it so hard, the disc goes too high. Streak tears after it, but what I see—and he doesn't—is that it's going to stall. Still, I think, it's got a chance. I've thrown it hard enough that it looks like it's just past the 40-yard mark. If it falls the right way and Streak can grab it...

The crowd hushes and Streak slows, staring up at the Frisbee, waiting for it to come down.

"Come on," I shout at the Frisbee.

The disc starts falling toward earth, but as I feared, it slips back toward me. Streak isn't expecting this, but he rushes after it.

"Jump, Streak! Jump!" I yell.

He lunges and the crowd gasps. Streak grabs the disc inches off the ground and then tumbles through the grass. All around me, students and adults go crazy, but it's not enough. The last catch is two points short. Brad and Shep win it, 14 points to 12.5.

Chapter Eleven

The next morning a chill fills Grandpa's house. *Fall is here,* I think, forcing myself from my cocoon of a bed. I dress, eat a quick bowl of cereal, and head outside. Overnight a leaf blizzard has struck and Grandpa has already informed me that I'm the clean-up crew.

I've never actually raked leaves before. In California we had one sycamore that lost its leaves every year, but it wasn't really enough to worry about. This morning, though, fallen leaves come up almost to my shins. I go to the shed and find a pair of gloves and a rake and dig in. I discover I kind of like doing it. I may not be able to control anything else in my life, but I can at least rake those leaves into submission. Besides, Streak has a great time diving into the leaf piles and tossing them into the air with his nose.

Raking also gives me a chance to think—and I've got a lot to figure out. I still haven't thought of a good topic for my paper on *Animal Farm.* I mean, the book isn't all that complicated:

1. People boss animals around.
2. Animals kick people off farm.
3. Pigs boss other animals around.
4. Pigs take place of people.
5. Everything's just as lousy as before.

What can I add to that? I don't know how Luke, Catherine, and the other kids come up with things to say about books.

"Well," I tell myself, adding to a big leaf pile near the front door, "the paper's not due for a week. I'll think of something."

Of course, I've got an even bigger problem than the paper—Brad. I kind of wish Streak had won the contest yesterday, but I'm glad he didn't, too. It probably would have made Brad madder than ever. On the other hand, I'm not sure that finishing second will make any difference.

I pause with the rake in my hand and straighten up. *Maybe,* I think, *Streak and I earned his respect with our performance yesterday and he'll quit using me as a spittoon.*

Then I mutter, "Yeah, dream on," and continue dragging the rake across the lawn.

Even after all the leaves are piled neatly around Grandpa's house, I'm still no closer to a solution. No matter how I look at it, I come up with only two options: either Brad is going to pound me to pulp *sooner,* or he's going to do it *later.*

* * *

The next morning I get to school as close to the bell as I can, but Brad finds me anyway. He doesn't shove me against the school wall. Instead he grinds me into a ponderosa pine. I try to appreciate the change of pace.

"Well, Butt Wipe," Brad growls. "Have a nice weekend?"

I know I should keep my mouth shut, but I can't. "You need to work on your sarcasm."

Brad flicks me painfully in the forehead with his middle finger. "You're...not...very...funny..." he growls, tapping out a new word with each flick.

I wince. "What do you want?"

"What I want is to know what the hell you thought you were doing Saturday? Did you think that wimpy dog of yours could beat me and Shep?"

This is the kind of comment I'm expecting, and my impulse is to chicken out and do my usual groveling. But all of a sudden I'm sick of this whole B.S. I'm sick of Brad. I'm sick of Big Sky Middle School. I'm fed up with this whole stinking place. Instead of cowering, I surprise myself.

I look Brad in the eyes. "You're damned right I thought Streak and I could beat you. I still do. You just got lucky last weekend."

Brad blinks and I can tell I've caught him off guard. He doesn't know whether to pulverize me with glee or try to defend his dog's honor. As his brain clunks and grinds searching for a response, I debate whether I should retreat and make a last stab at saving my skin.

But I realize I've come too far already and decide bolder is better.

"In fact," I tell him, "I'll make you a bet."

Brad and the Parasites laugh. "A bet? What do *you* have to bet?"

"Let go of me and I'll tell you."

Clunk. Sputter. Whir. Brad's walnut-sized brain commands him to release me. "Okay, Calf Crap, what do you want to bet?"

I straighten my shirt. I've got one more chance to chicken out, but I let it go. Instead, I hear myself asking, "Are you entering Shep in the city Frisbee contest next Saturday?"

Brad's eyes narrow. "Yeah. So what?"

"Well, I'm entering Streak, too."

I see Brad's eyes flash, but before he can say anything, I tell him, "My bet is that Streak and I beat you."

Brad laughs. "No way. We're going to kick your pansy California butts."

"You willing to back that up?" I ask, trying to sound confident.

Just then Luke shows up. "Guy," he says, tugging on his ear. "You ready to go to English?"

"In a minute," I tell him. "I'm making a bet with Brad."

Luke looks at me with alarm, then at Brad.

"What're you starin' at?" Brad growls at Luke. Then to me he says, "What's the bet?"

"Here it is. If Streak beats Shep, you have to leave Luke and me alone. No more morning wall sessions. No more snide remarks. It's hands off—forever."

"That's easy," Brad says. "Because you're going to *lose*. So what do I get when Shep wins and I get done grinding you into buffalo burger?"

"What you get," I tell him, thinking as fast as I can, "is a chance to graduate from Big Sky Middle School."

Brad snorts. "Yeah, that's a real good bet. Who says I even want to graduate?"

"Look around," I say. "This place is full of losers and you've already been here two extra years. You want to spend the rest of your life here?"

Brad glances at Clyde and Harold and I can hear the gears thudding and grinding in his cranium again. He jabs his finger into my chest. "So what? What can you do about it?"

"I can get you through math," I tell him.

Luke looks at me like one of those TV surgeons whose patient is slipping away on the operating table. I can tell he wants to save me, but he just doesn't know how.

"How can *you* get me through math?" Brad demands. Then his eyes light up. "You got answers to the tests?"

I shake my head. "No answers. But I can explain things to you so you can get them."

"He can," Luke volunteers. "He's helping me, too."

Brad's excitement fades and he spits on the ground. "Yeah, like no one's tried to do that before. Man, you're full of it. I don't give a crap about math, anyway."

I shrug. "It's up to you. That's the only class you need to get out of here. You want to stay here till they kick you out? You want to drop out and work at Burger Bite the rest of your life?"

I can tell I'm getting to him, but I also know that it's

not cool for a bully to want to do well in school—especially in front of his flunkies. So I play my last card.

"What's the matter?" I ask. "Afraid of what your little friends here think?"

Now I've made him mad and he grabs me by the shirt. "I'm not afraid of *anything*. And I'm especially not afraid of you and your wimpy dog."

"So," I say, forcing my voice to sound calm. "Is it a bet?"

Brad pushes me backward into the pine tree. "Damn right it's a bet—a bet you're going to lose!"

* * *

"Aw...do you know what you're doing?" Luke asks later that afternoon. He's throwing the Frisbee for Streak while I use the rake to bag up my leaf piles for pickup.

"No," I admit. "But what else was I going to do? I'm going to get ground into Quarter Pounders one way or another. Besides, don't you think Streak can do it?"

Luke throws the Frisbee again. "After Saturday, I know he can do it. I'm more worried about whether *you* can do it."

Annoyed, I set down the rake. "What does that mean?"

"Streak can catch anything as long as it's a good throw," he says. "The only reason he didn't win is because you were throwing them all over the place. Streak couldn't get to them."

I'm about to object, but realize he's right. "Well, what can I do about that? I was nervous."

"I know. That's why I'm thinking we've got to practice like it's a contest."

"You mean with other dogs?"

"Not with other dogs. We just need to mark out a field and time your throws. Maybe that'll get Streak more used to it, too."

"You think that'll help?"

Luke shrugs. "I don't know. But it's worth a try."

Chapter Twelve

As soon as I finish with the leaves, Luke and I walk to a nearby park with Streak. We don't have any white chalk, but I bring a tape measure and we use sticks to mark off a field more or less like the one at the Fall Fair. For the next hour—and every afternoon that week—we take Streak to the park and practice. Streak and I stand at the baseline. Luke hits the stopwatch function on his watch and yells, "Go!" and then we see how many points we can score in the next sixty seconds.

By the end of our first session, I'm forced to admit that Luke is right. Streak's not the problem. It's me. Even pretending that we're competing, I can feel my nerves hype up, and I almost always throw the first Frisbee way too far. Then I overcompensate and Streak ends up not knowing what to expect. With Luke coaching me, I try to concentrate on throwing the same way every time—just enough to clear the 30-yard line, but straight so Streak can tell where it's going.

The practice pays off. I find that if I just relax, I can count on five good throws in a minute. Every once in a while I squeeze in six, but usually only when I've screwed one up and it's fallen short. Anyway, by Wednesday Streak and I have twice scored 16.5 points and are consistently hitting between 13 and 15. I'm feeling pretty good about the bet by now, but I know that these practice sessions aren't the real thing.

And unfortunately, none of this helps me with my *Animal Farm* paper. Thursday afternoon I still don't have a clue what I'm going to write about. Luke and I do a short session with Streak, but then I tell Luke I've got to buckle down on English.

"You haven't even started your paper yet?" Luke asks, a look of horror on his face.

"No."

"Guy, it's due *tomorrow.*"

"I know. I know."

"Do you even know what you're going to write about?"

"I have some ideas," I lie.

"I hope they're fast ideas."

Back home, Streak and I find Mom home early, cooking spaghetti for dinner. She's hung Streak's second-place red ribbon on the wall over the kitchen table. "Were you out practicing?" she asks.

"Yeah," I say, sitting down across the table from Grandpa. Streak positions himself next to the oven and looks up at my mom as she sips spaghetti sauce from a wooden spoon.

"I knew that dog would do well!" Grandpa boasts. "He's got 'winner' written all over him."

Mom looks down at Streak. "And 'beggar' too. You aren't getting *any* of this sauce, so back off, mister."

Grandpa and I grin at each other, but Streak is too smart to believe my mom. He keeps staring.

"Guy, will you put the plates out?"

I get up to set the table.

"So when's the big competition?" Grandpa asks.

"This Saturday, at the Fairgrounds," I tell him.

"Boy, I would love to see that," Grandpa says. "If I can get my joints working, maybe I'll tool on down there."

After dinner I help my mom with the dishes. Streak finishes licking spaghetti sauce out of the saucepan and follows me to my room, settling down on the rug next to my feet. I sit at my desk for a while, but then flop onto my bed. I want to just lie there and rest for a while, but I'm too anxious about my report. The only good thing about the report is that it keeps me from worrying about Brad and the contest. Of course, pain is pain, no matter where it comes from.

"Why are teachers so obsessed with reports?" I grumble at Streak. "I read the book. Shouldn't that be enough?"

I decide I need some music to help me think. I sit up and start running my finger across my row of CDs. I've got them arranged alphabetically by group and chronologically by date of release.

"Creedence?" I ask myself. "No, too mellow. Led Zeppelin? Too wild. ZZ Top? Too funny."

Then, for some reason, my finger traces back to the Pink Floyd section and stops. My dad must've bought every Pink Floyd CD ever made, but I've only listened to a couple of them since he left. I like *Dark Side of the*

Moon and I love *The Wall,* but a lot of the others I remember only from my dad listening to them. Now, my eye lands on one in particular—*Animals.*

"I wonder what this one's like?" I ask Streak. He lifts his eyelids halfway and then re-closes them.

I pop the CD into my stereo, put on my headphones, and lie back down on my bed. I'd put the music on to get my mind off of the report, but now I catch myself really listening to the lyrics. By the middle of the second track, I can't believe what I'm hearing. It's already dark outside, so I flip on my desk light. Streak raises his head as I pull out the color sleeve that goes along with the CD. I open it and quickly find what I'm looking for—a complete copy of the lyrics.

I read through them carefully. When I'm finished, I start again. Then I head back to the bed and listen to the lyrics along with the music. As they unfold with David Gilmour's great guitar licks, it dawns on me. This album isn't about animals. It's about *Animal Farm!* I mean, it's not exactly the same, but they're so much alike it can't be a coincidence. If I have any doubts, the fourth song, "Sheep," clinches it:

What do you get for pretending the danger's not real.
Meek and obedient you follow the leader
Down well trodden corridors, into the valley of steel.
What a surprise!

Suddenly all kinds of images are flashing through my brain: Brad Mullen and the pigs from *Animal Farm;* the obedient students at Big Sky Middle School

103

slogging in straight lines through the school hallways; Principal Goode directing everyone like we don't have minds of our own.

I leap off my bed, turn on my Mac, and start typing.

* * *

The next day, my head feels full of mud. I stagger to school and find Luke sitting on the front steps. Brad and the Parasites strut by and Brad shoots me an I'm-gonna-kick-your-ass look, but fortunately he's been leaving me alone since our bet. I'm sure he's saving it up so he can give me a *really* good beating tomorrow after the contest.

"Aw...you look terrible," Luke says. "Are you sick?"

"No more than usual," I tell him. "I only slept a couple of hours last night."

Luke shakes his head as we push through the school's front doors. "I told you not to wait until the last second to do that paper."

"I can't help it," I say. "I always write reports at the last second."

"Did you come up with an idea?"

"Sort of, but Mrs. Minneman will probably hate it."

We walk into English as the other kids are making their way to their seats.

"Hello, Guy," I hear a familiar voice say, and I'm stunned to find Catherine looking at me. I have to admit that since the Fall Fair I've been avoiding her—especially after she stood up to Brad and I didn't. But the sound of her voice sends familiar flutters through my stomach.

"Oh, uh, hi," I say, accidentally smacking my thigh into a desk.

"How are you doing?" she asks.

"I'm, uh, okay."

"How's Streak doing?"

"He's good. Real good."

"You're entering the contest tomorrow?"

"Yeah, uh, why?" I ask.

"I wanted to make sure, so I can come watch."

"You're coming?"

"Sure. The whole school's going to be there. Everyone knows about your bet."

The fluttering in my stomach is replaced by punching fists. I glance at Luke, who's eavesdropping from his desk. He shrugs like he doesn't know a thing about it.

"They are? I mean, they do?" I ask.

"Yes. If you don't mind me saying so, the bet's pretty dumb. But don't worry. I'm sure you're going to win—and most people are rooting for you."

As Mrs. Minneman asks everyone to take their seats, Catherine flashes me a dazzling smile. I sink down into my chair, my skin suddenly feeling as hot as a chrome door handle in July. I again look at Luke.

"I didn't tell anyone," he whispers. "I swear. It must have been Brad or the Parasites."

Whoever spread the news, this is bad. I'm going to be nervous enough just competing against Brad. Now, with the whole school watching...

Mrs. Minneman clears her throat, and Luke and I face forward.

"As you know," Mrs. Minneman says, "your papers on *Animal Farm* are due today. Did anyone have any trouble?"

Half a dozen kids grumble, but no one comes right out and admits it.

"Great!" Mrs. Minneman says way too cheerfully. "Then I'd appreciate it if you would all hand them forward."

I reach into my backpack and pull out my notebook. I remove my paper, which is seven pages long even though Mrs. Minneman only asked for three. On the title page it reads "Animal Farm Middle School, by Guy Martinez." As I pass the paper forward, I glance at it one last time and see that I misspelled "animal" as "aminal" in the very first sentence. I have no doubt I'll get another D on it and I wonder again what got into me last night. I'm so tired, I can barely remember. All I recall is listening to the CD over and over, then having this brainstorm to compare the book *Animal Farm* to the social structure of Big Sky Middle School. Five hours later—at two A.M.—I'd written seven pages.

Geez, I wonder what was in Mom's spaghetti?

Chapter Thirteen

The next morning, the plan is for Luke to come over to my house at nine. Then my mom will drive us to the Fairgrounds for the city Frisbee meet. I get out of bed early to warm up Streak and I only give him a half ration of dog food so he's not too weighted down for the contest. Grandpa has decided not to come because of his arthritis. Mom gets him squared away with V8 juice and by nine o'clock, we're ready to go.

There's only one problem: Luke doesn't show.

At 9:10 my mom says, "Give him a call. Maybe something came up."

"I don't think so," I tell her. "Luke is always on time." But I try his number anyway and get the answering machine.

"Well, maybe he thought we were picking him up in front of his house," Mom suggests. "Come on. Let's go over there."

"Mom, I don't even know where he lives."

She looks at me. "You don't? I thought you'd been over there lots of times."

I shake my head. "No. He always came up with some reason why we shouldn't."

"Oh." My mom doesn't say anything for a second. Then she walks into the kitchen and I follow. Grandpa is sitting by the window, watching a couple of crows in the backyard.

"Those crows," he says, "are the smartest birds God ever put his mind into making. Did I ever tell you about the crow that picked the lock on my shed?"

"Dad," my mother says. "Do you know where Luke's house is?"

"You mean Daniel's grandson?"

"That's the one."

"Oh, well, they used to live over on Jefferson. The 600 block, I think. Maybe 620?"

My mom gives Grandpa a kiss. "Thanks, Dad. We'll be back in a couple of hours."

"Go get 'em!" Grandpa hollers at Streak and me.

* * *

We drive over to Jefferson Street in the Honda. Mom waits in the car while Streak and I go knock on a couple of doors. Finally I find the right house. Grandpa wasn't far off. The address is 632, a green bungalow set back a little from the street. The lawn is mowed and the leaves are raked, but the paint's chipping off the wooden siding. I can tell the place needs work.

I go up to the door and press the doorbell. I don't hear a ring, so I knock real loudly and wait.

Nothing.

I knock again and still there's no answer.

A woman with gardening gloves appears around the corner. I jump, startled, but Streak prances up to her. "Can I help you with anything?" she asks.

"Uh, yeah. I'm looking for Luke. Is he around?"

The woman's face grows serious. "Oh, didn't you hear?"

"Hear what?" I ask, confused.

"About Luke's father. He had a stroke last night and the ambulance came and took him to Community Hospital."

This is the last thing I expect. Even though I have no idea how old Luke's parents are, I picture them about my mom's age. How could his dad have a stroke?

"Uh, is he okay?" I ask.

"I'm sorry. I haven't heard," the woman says. "But if you see him, tell him Sophie and her family send their love. And tell him not to worry. We're looking after the place."

"Yeah, thanks," I say, barely listening. "Come on, Streak."

We walk back to the Honda and climb in.

"What is it?" my mom asks. "Wasn't that Luke's house?"

"Yeah," I say. "His dad's had a stroke."

"Oh no. Is he all right?"

"I don't know. That woman said they took him to Community Hospital."

We sit there for a moment. Then my mom asks, "What do you want to do?"

I'm a little surprised she asks. I'm used to her just

taking charge of situations like this. But I go ahead and bend my brain to the question. My first impulse is to go straight to the hospital. On the other hand, I've got a bet with a bully, and if I don't show up for the contest—well, I don't even like to think about it. It's not just Brad I'm going to have to face. It's the rest of Big Sky Middle School, too.

Streak licks me on the ear from the backseat. I tell my mom, "Let's go to the hospital."

As we pull away from the curb, I wonder: Does the FBI have a Witness Protection Program for wimps?

* * *

The last time I entered a hospital was when I was five years old and some slasher-movie doctor ripped my tonsils out. What I mostly remember about the experience is eating green Jell-O and getting a new stuffed animal—I think it was a penguin. That's a long way of saying I have no idea what to do when my mom and I walk through the sliding glass doors and are confronted by a large waiting room and a wraparound counter. The counter is staffed by two busy-looking receptionists or nurses, I can't tell which.

I ask my mom to go ahead and take Streak home. Grandpa's house is only about a mile from the hospital and I can easily walk it after I'm done doing whatever it is I'm going to do here.

"Are you sure?" she asks me.

I nod.

"Okay, honey," she says, giving my shoulder a

squeeze. "Tell Luke that Grandpa and I are thinking about him."

After my mom leaves, I clear my throat and one of the receptionists looks up at me. "Can I help you?" she asks, making clear that's the last thing she's interested in doing.

"Well, I want to...I mean, I'm here to see a friend. His dad's—"

"Name?" the woman demands.

"Luke Grant," I tell her.

She punches in the name on the computer. "That's the patient's name?"

"No. I don't know his dad's name."

"Well, that won't help us, will it now?" Snorting impatiently, she flips through some names on the screen. "Grant. Here it is. He's in neurology. Follow the red lines on the floor."

"Thanks," I tell her, though I feel like telling her to get some Preparation H. She needs it way more than Grandpa does.

The red line leads me to an elevator and up to the fourth floor. From there I continue following the line around several corners and through two or three double swinging doors. In no time I'm lost.

I stop at a nurse's station and a woman much friendlier than the receptionist points me toward the hospital's south wing.

I head down a short hallway and spot Luke sitting alone on a couch. I take a deep breath and walk up to him.

"Hi."

Luke looks up. "Guy... What are you doing here? What about...?"

I sit down next to him. "I heard about your dad. Is he okay?"

Luke, the most stable, unflappable kid I've ever met, looks like he's been hit by a tidal wave. His eyes fill with water and tears crawl down his cheeks. I spot a Kleenex box on a nearby table and retrieve it.

He takes one and blows his nose. Then he uses another to wipe off his face.

"Sorry," he says.

I wave off his apology. "So what's going on?" I ask him.

"He had a stroke," Luke says.

"What is that, exactly?"

"A blood vessel in his brain broke."

"Is it bad?"

Luke shakes his head. "They don't know. It's going to be a while before... My mom's in there with him now."

Luke pulls out another Kleenex and again blows his nose.

We sit for a minute and I glance around the waiting room. It's small, filled with chairs and couches with vinyl-covered foam cushions. A coffee machine sits on a corner table next to a stack of magazines. The alcohol hospital smell stings my nostrils.

I debate whether to ask Luke any more questions, but he speaks up first.

"The last few years have been real hard on my dad," he starts to explain.

"Has he been sick?"

Luke shakes his head and thinks for a moment. "Have you ever heard of the Ponderosa Creek Gold Mine?"

I search my memory. Grandpa did mention something about a gold mine, but that name doesn't sound familiar. "Not really," I tell Luke.

"That's because there isn't one. Four years ago, a big mining company came in and wanted to build a cyanide-leach pit mine in Ponderosa Canyon."

"Cyanide-leach pit mine? What's that?" I ask. In my history classes in California I'd read about the gold rush and gold panning and all that, but I never heard about pit mines.

"It's a kind of mining where they dig out the ore, crush it, and extract the gold using cyanide."

"Geez... That doesn't sound...good."

Luke shakes his head. "The cyanide gets into the water, kills the fish and wildlife, and poisons wells. It causes all kinds of birth defects in humans, too. The mine company said they'd protect the environment and everything, but no other gold mining company has ever kept its word about that. They go into a place, take the gold, and leave behind a disaster. It happens over and over again."

"That sucks. So why do people let them do it?" I ask.

"The economy's so bad in Montana, people are willing to believe almost anything. If a mine company comes in and says they'll give everyone high-paying jobs and protect the environment, nobody wants to look too hard at whether they're lying or not."

Luke stops talking and I turn this over in my head.

"So what's this got to do with your dad?" I finally ask.

"When the mine company came in," Luke continues, "they held a town meeting. The man from the mine company made a big speech about their plans and everyone clapped. But then my dad stood up and started asking questions. He'd been doing research on this company and found out they'd poisoned rivers and streams all over North America. He caught them in their lies. After the meeting, he wrote letters to the newspapers and contacted the Montana Rivers Coalition and other environmental groups about the project."

"Well, weren't people glad to find out the truth?" I ask.

Luke shakes his head again. "No. When the mine got canceled, everyone blamed my dad. He had his own veterinary practice before, but people quit bringing their animals and it just dribbled away to nothing. My mom had a good job at the credit union, and they made up an excuse to fire her."

"That's terrible."

"My dad got death threats, too. Someone blew up our mailbox. Then..."

I see Luke's eyes well up again and I tell him, "You don't have to say any more."

"Aw...I wanted to tell you anyway." He stares blankly down the corridor for a moment, then goes on with his story.

"One morning I went outside to get the paper and I found both of our dogs dead on the front lawn. Someone had picked them up, shot them, and dumped them."

My heart falls through my stomach.

"You're kidding..." I mutter, and think to myself, *What kind of person could do something like that?* I don't have to think long to come up with the answer—an older version of Brad Mullen.

"Anyway," Luke says, his nose still dripping, "my dad never really got over it. He thought he was doing something good for the town and the community. But instead of thanking him, they turned on him. My mom finally found work over at the Hi-Lo grocery store, but it's been hard to make ends meet and my dad's been depressed a lot, always blaming himself for what happened. I guess it finally got to be too much."

I nod. A lot of missing pieces suddenly fit into place—why Luke is a loner at school and gets picked on by Brad. Why Luke never invites me over to his house. Why he knows so much about animals. Why he doesn't have any pets and why he's so crazy about Streak. I put my hand on his shoulder and he looks at me and manages a smile. Then it vanishes.

"Aw...Guy. What about the Frisbee contest?"

I shrug. "Forget it. I didn't care about it anyway." It's a lie, but I'm glad I came to the hospital. Monday...well, maybe I'll feel different.

Chapter Fourteen

T hat night I wake up every hour, my mind racing. I finally give up trying to sleep at about 6:30 Sunday morning and get up to take Streak for a walk.

After yesterday, I understand a lot more about what's going on in this town. Now, the Frisbee contest and my bet with Brad don't seem so important. Now, I'm ready for a fight. As I walk, I swing my fists, landing blows into Brad's imaginary moronic face, hopping from side to side as I dodge his feeble counterpunches. Streak looks at me curiously and jumps up, thinking it's a new kind of game, but I ignore him. I'm serious with a capital *S*.

When we get back to Grandpa's house, I'm pretty sure no one else is up, but I open the door quietly just in case. I swing my fist into one last uppercut as I walk into the kitchen. Too late, I spot Grandpa sitting at the *That '70s Show* table, reading the morning paper.

I halt, flat-footed.

"Look who's up," Grandpa says in his raspy morning voice.

"Uh, I couldn't sleep," I explain, wondering if he noticed me swinging my fist.

"What?" he says, turning up his hearing aid.

"I didn't sleep well," I say a little louder.

I pour Streak his cup of dry dog food. My stomach is rumbling and I'd like a bowl of cereal, but I don't feel like getting into a long conversation with Grandpa so I start toward my room. My move doesn't work.

"Hold on, son!" Grandpa says. "Don't be in such a rush. Sit down and tell me about your plans for the day."

I turn halfway around. "Not much to tell."

"You going to go visit Luke's dad at the hospital?"

"I'm not sure he can have visitors yet," I say, still hoping I can slip away without a conversation.

"Yeah, that wouldn't surprise me after a stroke. Any news on how he's doing?"

I shake my head and again start for my room. Grandpa again stops me.

"Well," he croaks, "tell me what you *are* going to do, then. Just so's I have something to think about."

While Streak crunches away on his food, I reluctantly pull up a chair across from Grandpa.

"I don't know," I say. "Maybe do some homework. Listen to some music."

"Where'd you go on your walk?" Grandpa asks.

I shrug. "Just around."

"For just walking around, you sure picked up a lot of baggage. I haven't seen a boy so tied-down-looking since I was in the Service."

I don't say anything.

"What's eatin' you, son?" Grandpa asks. "Sometimes it helps to spill it—especially to a senile old fart who won't remember it long enough to blab to anyone."

I smile despite myself. "It's nothing. This town just sucks. That's all."

Grandpa grins and nods. "I suppose you're right. It probably does. Then again, every place sucks sometimes. If you'd stuck around California long enough, you'd a found that out."

"I didn't get much of a chance," I say, unable to keep the bitterness out of my voice.

"No. No, you didn't. We all get lassoed into things we don't count on."

I look Grandpa in the eye. "Grandpa, did you know what happened to Luke's family with that gold mine?"

Grandpa folds up the newspaper and leans back in his chair. "I suppose I had a good idea."

"Why didn't you tell me about it?"

Grandpa pauses. "Well, I figured Luke's got a right to his own business."

"How could people here have done that to him and his family?"

"It wasn't everyone, son. Some people were behind Luke's dad. They just didn't speak up as loudly as the others. Those others, they got pretty mean-spirited—especially when they thought they were going to get rich and didn't."

"Whose side were you on?"

Grandpa pauses a moment. "I admired what Luke's dad was doing, but I kept quiet like a lot of other folks. 'Course now, I wish I'd done more, but 20/20 hindsight is about as useful as a legless horse. It won't get you anywhere."

"It's not right."

"No, it's not. But it's not the last time you'll come across something ugly in your life. All you can do is try to make the right decisions yourself and hope that people will come around. That's what Luke's dad did."

"And he paid for it."

Grandpa slowly nods. "Yep. I suppose he did."

I get up and again start out of the kitchen.

"Guy?" my grandfather says.

I turn and look at him.

"Son, I'm not exactly sure what you got planned. But if those imaginary punches are any indication, don't wait till he comes to you. Take it to him. And make sure it's a surprise."

I just stand and stare at Grandpa. Though I don't want to admit it, I can see in his eyes that he's two steps ahead of me.

"Thanks," I mutter.

As I move off, Grandpa holds up the newspaper and says, "By the way, did you see that Brad and his dog finished first in the competition yesterday? Looks like he'll be going to Regionals in Missoula next weekend."

* * *

The next morning I leave for school a few minutes early. Instead of going to the front of the school as usual, I head for a small park across the street and half a block away. A single cottonwood grows in the middle of the park. The kids call it the Smoking Tree because that's where all the smokers hang out. It's also where Brad and the Parasites spend their time when they're not in detention, and sure enough, I spot them now, standing near a big trash can that looks like someone's been whaling on it with a sledgehammer. My heart starts beating faster, but as I walk toward Brad and his crew, I remind myself of all the crap I've had to take from them.

When I'm twenty yards away, Clyde Crookshank notices me, takes a puff on a cigarette, and says something to Brad. Brad turns and my hands clench tight. I've decided I'm not going to talk or trade insults or anything. I'm just going to take Grandpa's advice and let him have it.

"Well," Brad sneers, "if it isn't the California cop-out."

I walk closer, breathing heavily. My ears ring from the blood pounding through them. I'm almost within striking distance and I can see Brad isn't expecting a thing. One more step and—

"Guy, wait!"

I stop in my tracks. Brad and the Parasites look beyond my shoulder and I turn to see Luke galloping toward me.

"What are you doing here?" I ask.

"Yeah, what are you *both* doing here?" Brad spits. "This place is off-limits to losers." He's holding a packet of Red Man chewing tobacco, and he pulls out a fresh wad and shoves it into his cheek. "You think you can talk your way out of chickening out Saturday?"

Harold Dicks makes a clucking sound.

"It's...it's my fault Guy wasn't there," Luke says, panting after his sprint across the park. "My dad got sick and Guy came to the hospital."

"That figures," says Harold. "Your dad's a wimp, just like you."

I step toward him. "You better watch it, Dicks."

Brad grabs me by the front of my shirt and jerks me back. "*You'd* better watch it, Calf Crap. Or have you forgotten your place around here?"

My hands clench again, but Luke cuts in. "Aw...wait, you guys. I've got good news."

Brad and I glare at each other and he lets go of my shirt.

"Mr. Harrington—the man in charge of the city competition—used to bring his dogs to my dad's clinic," Luke continues. "Yesterday I called him up to explain what happened on Saturday—you know, about you and Streak missing the contest and all. I told him you wouldn't have missed it if it hadn't been for me."

"So?" Brad says. "A bet's a bet and you lost. It's payback time."

"That's what I'm saying," Luke goes on, barely pausing for a breath. "Mr. Harrington talked to the officials from Gulp Pet Foods, and they said Streak can still compete in the regional Frisbee championship this weekend in Missoula. This year, they added a qualifying round the day of the regional competition. It's mostly for people in rural areas who can't get to other matches, but they said Streak can do it, too. All Streak has to do is get 10 points in the qualifying round and they'll let him enter the main event.

"So," Luke finishes, looking completely winded, "you guys can still do your bet."

"Who says I *want* to do that?" Brad says. "As far as I'm concerned, California and his lame-ass dog lost."

The Parasites snicker.

"What's the matter?" I ask Brad. "Are you afraid Streak and I are going to win next weekend?"

Brad puffs up his chest and jabs his finger into my collarbone. "I'm not afraid of anything—especially not you, Calf Crap!" As he talks, flecks of tobacco juice hit my face. I'm on the verge of smashing my fist into his ugly mug, but I hold back. I can see I'm getting to him.

"Okay, then. Will you do it if we sweeten the bet?" I ask.

Brad stops chewing and his eyes narrow. "How?"

I wish I have more time to come up with something, but I blurt out, "If I lose, I'll buy your chewing tobacco for a month. If you lose, you've got to quit bullying everyone in the school. *And* you've got to shave Shep's fur...and your own head."

Tapeworm and Maggot seem to get a big kick out of this idea and laugh, but Brad shoots them a laser stare and they clam up.

"That's a great idea," Luke whispers to me.

Brad takes a couple more chews on his Red Man and spits. I can hear those gears grinding in his head. Finally he says, "You're on."

Luke and I both breathe sighs of relief and start to turn away.

"But..." Brad growls.

I turn back toward him and see a sly smirk spread

across his face. "But," he says, "I've already got enough tobacco. If I agree to quit giving you wimps a hard time and shave my head, I get something better on my end."

"What?" I ask, knowing I'm not going to like it.

Brad takes a couple of chews. Then he says slowly, "If I win, I get your damn dog."

"Streak?" Luke says.

I don't say anything. This is the last thing I expect Brad to come up with.

"What's the matter?" Clyde Crookshank jeers. "You scared?" Harold Dicks starts making clucking sounds again.

"I'm not scared," I say and, at least for the moment, I mean it. But he's got to be crazy if he thinks I'm going to bet my dog.

"No way," I tell him.

"I figured you'd wimp out." Then Brad says something that hits me like a sucker punch. "I hear that your dad thought you were such a coward, he couldn't even stand to be around you."

At the mention of my dad my head suddenly fills with the sounds of grinding ice. For a moment I can't even talk. Then I croak, "Leave my family out of it."

But Brad smells blood. "You know it's true, Calf Crap. Your dad was so sick of you, he took off and left you and your mom alone."

"Watch it," I warn him. I try desperately to retreat behind my internal castle walls, but Brad has me trapped.

"Careful now," he hisses. "You don't have a girl to stand up for you this time."

My vision is swirling with red and purple and all I can think of is getting Brad to stop saying the things he's saying.

"Shut up!" I shout at him.

"Ooh, look who's upset!" Harold snickers.

"Just shut up!" I yell again, louder. Everyone around the Smoking Tree is staring at us.

Brad steps closer to me and I can feel his hot breath on my face. "I'll shut up if you make the bet."

I want to respond, but I can't. I have no words. I don't have *anything*.

"Come on," Brad taunts. "Make the bet. Or if you'd like, I can tell everyone all about what a—"

"Fine!" The word leaps out of my mouth.

Luke gasps. "Guy!"

Brad spits. Then he steps back and grins. "Good. I always wanted a Border collie. Now I'm going to get one."

Chapter Fifteen

As Luke and I walk toward the school, my vision is still swirling and my body trembles.

Luke gapes at me, also in shock. "Aw...Guy, are you sure about this?"

I shake my head, unable to talk. And slowly the realization of what I've done sinks in.

"Guy," Luke says. "You just bet *Streak.*"

I swallow, trying to get some saliva back into my mouth. "I know."

"You wouldn't let Brad have him. *Would you?*"

As we climb the front stairs of the school, I struggle to get control of myself. "I...I don't...know. Don't you think we'll win?" I ask Luke.

"Sure you'll win," says Luke. "At least I'm pretty sure you will."

It's not the gushing enthusiasm I'm looking for.

Luke's face almost drags across the floor. "This is my fault," he says.

"No..." I say, but I feel so bad myself, I can't offer him anything more.

We shuffle into English class and I take my seat. Catherine turns and says hello. She looks like she wants to ask me a question, but I avoid her eyes. I want to crawl under a rock. Or better yet, under a manure pile. That's where I belong. How could I have bet my dog with a guy whose closest relative is a Neanderthal?

But what bothers me almost as much as the actual bet is what Brad said. He really got to me about my dad. I didn't think anyone could do that anymore. I thought I'd dealt with my father leaving, sealed it away as just one of those terrible things that happen and you get used to. Now I realize I was wrong. In an instant Brad ripped away my best defenses, leaving me completely exposed. Like anything could come along and...obliterate me.

To make the day perfect, Mrs. Minneman hands out yet another novel for us to read. This one's called *Fahrenheit 451* by a guy named Ray Bradbury. Orange flames fill the book's cover.

I stare at them, wishing they would burn me into nothing.

* * *

The week begins its painful crawl toward Saturday and the regional Frisbee meet. I don't tell my mom or Grandpa about my bet, but Grandpa looks slightly relieved when I come home without a broken nose after school on Monday. I can barely look at Streak, I feel so guilty, but Luke recovers his good attitude and tries to help me put a positive spin on things. And I tell myself that if he can do that with what his family's been through, I can somehow get through this thing with Brad. I don't know how, but there's got to be some way.

After school on Tuesday, Luke and I take Streak to the park and give him a good workout. Luke doesn't stay as long as usual because he has to go to the hospital to visit his dad, but Streak and I keep at it until it starts getting dark.

Unfortunately, on Wednesday the weather turns from autumn-chilly to butt-freezing cold. By the time we get to the park a northern wind is screaming down from Canada and the icy air turns my fingers to stone. Streak loves it and bounces around like a SuperBall, but I'm wearing every sweater and sweatshirt I own and still feel like an igloo.

"I hear it's supposed to snow by the weekend," Luke tells me, taking a turn with the Frisbee while I try to thaw out my frozen fingers. He's obviously not as bothered by the cold as I am. "A big front's coming in."

"Do you think they'll cancel the contest?" I ask, rubbing my hands together.

"Aw...Guy, this is Montana, remember?"

"Does that mean no?"

"They might cancel if there's a couple of feet of snow on the ground. But we hardly ever get that much this early in the season."

I'm disappointed, but we start in on our workout session. Luke walks to the sideline of our Frisbee field and yells, "Go!"

I start throwing the disc. Streak flies after it like this is what he lives for. *In a way he does,* I think with yet another stab of guilt. He chases them down, one after another. He only misses the ones I screw up and I realize that both of us have gotten about as good at this as we're going to get.

After four or five trial runs, we stop for a rest. With the exercise, my core body temperature has risen from sub-freezing back up to forty or fifty degrees.

"Hey, how's your dad doing?" I ask Luke. He hasn't mentioned anything for a couple of days now.

A small smile turns the corners of Luke's mouth. "Aw...he's doing better. The doctors say we got him to the hospital in time. He might have a little trouble with his left arm and his speech, but he's going to be okay. He'll be able to come home this weekend."

"That's great," I say, meaning it.

Then a cloud passes over Luke's face.

"What's wrong?" I ask him.

"Well, uh..."

I wait. Luke doesn't usually have trouble talking, so I'm guessing it's something bad.

"It's just that..."

"Yeah?"

"My parents are talking about moving."

I don't get it at first. "You mean to another house?"

Luke shakes his head. "Moving from Coffee."

A lead weight drops into my small intestine. "What do you mean? What are you talking about?"

"Aw... Since my dad's stroke, they're saying they might be ready for a change. They said they've always wanted to move to Washington or Oregon."

"When?" I say, my voice cracking.

Luke shrugs. "Maybe after Christmas."

The weight in my intestines gets heavier. I can't believe what Luke's saying. I mean, I finally find a good friend in this town and now he's going to leave? This can't be happening.

"Can't you talk them into staying?" I ask.

"I already tried. Anyway, it's not for sure yet," Luke adds, trying to make me feel better. "That kind of reminds me. I was wondering if I could ask a favor."

I watch Streak as he sniffs at some squirrel poop near a chestnut tree. "Sure," I mumble, still reeling from the bombshell he's dropped. "What is it?"

* * *

Twenty minutes later, Streak and I are waiting outside a service door at the back of Community Hospital. The door opens and Luke silently motions us in. With Streak on his lead we tiptoe into a large room packed with cardboard boxes.

"It's a good thing Streak doesn't bark," I tell Luke. "Are you sure about this?"

Luke looks at me. "No."

We both stifle laughs and already I'm feeling better about what he told me about moving. Luke said it wasn't a sure thing, after all. Also, once his dad recovers maybe he'll realize what a huge hassle moving is. The more I think about it, the more I convince myself that they'll end up changing their minds.

Luke leads Streak and me up a back stairwell of the hospital. He obviously knows his way around and when we reach the fourth floor, he whispers, "Wait here. I'll make sure it's clear."

He eases the door open and steps out. A moment later, he's back. "Okay. Let's go."

I feel my heart pounding, but in an excited way. Following Luke, we sneak down a couple of hallways and slip around corners. Streak wants to stop and sniff everything, but I pull him along before he pees on a wall or some million-dollar piece of equipment. Finally we reach a door marked "440" and Luke opens it. Inside, I see a woman sitting in a chair. She's talking to a man propped up in a hospital bed.

Luke goes in and Streak tugs me in after him. The woman stands up.

"Luke," she says, "what are you *doing?*"

"Mom," he says. "This is my friend Guy. And we brought a special visitor along. This is Streak."

The woman's face immediately softens. Streak sniffs the hem of her pants and she extends her hand to me. "Glad to meet you finally, Guy. Luke's told me all about you and what you've been doing for him. He's lucky to have a friend like you." She bends over and scratches Streak's ears. "And lucky to have you, too!"

Streak wags his stump.

"Oh, uh, thanks," I mumble. "Nice to meet you." But I'm thinking that Streak and I are the lucky ones.

"And Guy," Luke continues, "this is my dad."

Luke's father is almost a spitting image of Luke, but

I can't believe how old he looks. His hair is almost completely gray, and wrinkles run like little canyons around his eyes and mouth. Life's definitely taken a chunk out of this guy.

The man starts to lift his hand to shake, but before he can, Streak leaps onto the bed.

"Streak!" I shout. "Streak, off. Right now!"

But Luke's father's eyes sparkle and he waves away my commands. Now I understand why Luke wanted me to bring Streak. As Streak plants a paw on the man's chest and licks his cheeks, twenty years seem to fall off Luke's dad's face. He's obviously been missing animals way too long.

"Glad to meet you, Guy. And Streak." Luke's dad speaks slowly and with effort, but he doesn't appear to be in any pain. He pets Streak and Streak settles down and lets him, almost as if he understands that Luke's dad isn't well.

"Well, uh, glad to meet you, too," I say and we all laugh.

We stay for about fifteen minutes, mostly talking about dogs and school and stuff like that. Finally Luke's mom says, "You know, Luke, having pets in here is really *not*—"

Just then the door to the room bursts open and a woman with short brown hair and a stethoscope stands in front of us.

Streak leaps off the bed and the doctor jumps back.

"Streak, no!" Luke and I both shout at the same time, but Streak is too keyed up. He starts licking the doctor's feet and I see a series of expressions shoot over her face: surprise, fear, anger, and—fortunately—amusement.

Composing herself, the doctor says, "I must have the wrong hospital. I didn't realize I was at the veterinary clinic."

We all laugh nervously as the woman bends down to scratch Streak behind the ears. "And who might this be?"

"Aw...that's Streak," Luke says. "It's my fault he's in here. I just thought..."

As Luke struggles to finish, the doctor stands up and says, "I think I understand. But if the nurses catch you in here, I can't be responsible for their actions."

The doctor says this in good humor, but Luke and I take the hint. We thank the doctor and say good-bye to Luke's parents. Before we leave, Luke's dad says, "Good luck...with Streak...Saturday."

"Thanks," I say. "We'll need it."

Heading home, all Luke says is "Thanks, Guy."

I shrug. "It was fun."

We walk a few minutes and I get an idea. "You know, your dad should start up his practice again here in Coffee. I bet people would come. Five years is a long time and this place seems to have animals out the wazoo." *Also,* I think, *it would keep Luke here in Coffee with me.*

"Aw...I think so too," says Luke. "I've told my dad before. So has my mom, but he keeps saying he's not ready to do vet work again. Maybe after this, he'll change his mind..."

* * *

That night I try to study for a social studies test, but my mind keeps wandering off to Luke and his family. Man, I sure hope they don't decide to leave. I mean, I know it's been bad for them, but isn't there a chance they could get things right again?

Thinking about Luke also makes me think about my own family—and face something for the first time. Even though we moved all the way to Montana, I guess in the back of my mind, I've kept hoping my dad would suddenly show up and make everything better again. Now, I'm finally figuring out that's not going to happen. Not to me. Not to Luke, either. Sometimes crappy things happen and they don't ever get fixed. You just have to keep breathing and hope that someday they'll stop hurting as much.

But that doesn't mean you can't try to keep crappy things from happening in the first place. I look down at Streak lying on the floor next to me and for the thousandth time wonder how I could have bet him on a stupid contest. I tell myself I was upset and I didn't know what I was doing, but that doesn't make me feel any better.

What if we lose? I wonder. *Is it even conceivable I'd give Brad my dog?*

I slam my social studies book closed and hope there's some angle, somewhere, I've been overlooking.

Chapter Sixteen

The weather worsens through the rest of the week. By Saturday morning, when my mom and I are eating breakfast, fluffy white flakes are drifting down from the sky.

Mom is excited to see it. "Wow, I haven't seen real snow like this in twenty years, since I moved away from here! Isn't it neat, Guy?"

I grunt and shove a last bite of cereal in my mouth.

"Come on, let's see some enthusiasm!" my mom says. "You've seemed down all week. Isn't the snow cool?"

"I'm just worried about the contest," I say, which is technically true, though I haven't dared tell her about my bet with Brad—and what's really at stake.

"Oh," she says. "Well, if anyone deserves to win, it's you. I've been impressed by how hard you've been practicing."

"We'd better get going," I say, switching subjects.

We say good-bye to Grandpa, and the three of us— my mom, Streak, and I—get into the Honda. We pick up Luke and pull onto the highway for the eighty-mile trek to Missoula. For the first time, Mom seems concerned about the weather.

"You're the expert, Luke," she says, turning on her wipers to brush away the flakes. "Is it going to get worse?"

"It'll be okay," Luke says. "You have chains, don't you?"

Mom and I look at each other. "Chains?" I ask.

"You know, to put on your tires in the snow. They give you better traction."

This is the first I've ever heard of them. "We don't have chains, do we, Mom?"

"I was going to get some the next time I got paid," she says, "but..."

"Aw...we'll be okay," Luke assures her. "This is nothing. Yet."

"Besides," my mom says, "we've got Streak. If we run into trouble, we'll just hitch him up and sled along behind."

Luke and I chuckle politely, and I look around at the landscape. The highway cuts through a narrow valley bordered by pine- and fir-covered mountains. A scenic river meanders alongside the road, but I know that this area's pretty dry. A few inches less rainfall each year and this would probably be desert—at least, that's what Grandpa's always saying.

As we get closer to Missoula I can feel my adrenaline pick up. In addition to my nervousness about the contest, I've only been to Missoula once before, when we were moving up here last summer. By California standards, it's puny—about the size of an L.A. suburb. But it's Montana's second-largest city and I find myself looking forward to seeing civilization again. After an hour, we drive through one last canyon and the town spreads out before us. Luke points out the landmarks.

"There's the University of Montana over there," Luke tells us, motioning to the left. "See that big *M* up on the mountain? That marks Mount Sentinel."

Streak eagerly wags his stump and tries to work his way up to the front seat with Mom and me. "Back!" I tell him. He scoots back with Luke for a moment, but then makes another stab at the front.

"I guess he's excited about seeing the city, too," Mom says with a chuckle.

By the time we pull off the interstate, snow is beginning to stick to the road. The qualifying round of the contest isn't scheduled to start until two o'clock, though, and we've got plenty of time. Mom takes us to a local fast-food place called Del's for an early lunch. Then, about noon, we head toward the fairgrounds.

When we arrive, we discover that the Frisbee contest is only a small part of the day. A full-on dog show is underway, and Luke gets as keyed up as the dogs that are yipping and yapping around us. "Aw...come on!" he says. "Let's look around."

"Go ahead," Mom tells us. "I'm going to snoop through the crafts displays."

I put Streak on his lead and Luke and I start making the rounds. Man, I've never seen so many different breeds of dogs. I recognize a few—retrievers, black

Labs, beagles—but a lot of them look like mutant experiments from another planet. Streak's in heaven. He sniffs every dog tail in sight and pees on anything resembling a fence post. Most of the dog owners don't mind, but some look pretty huffy about it, as if to say, "How dare you let such an uncouth beast sniff my dog's derriere!"

The show buzzes with events. We pass a big sign announcing a competition for basic obedience skills. In another area, it looks like they're giving prizes for well-groomed dogs. Then we get to the best part.

"Look at that!" Luke exclaims.

Up ahead, we see a large ring full of man-made obstacles. As we draw near, an official shouts, "Go!" and a Border collie and his owner rush out to the beginning of the course. Running alongside her dog, the owner barks commands and the Border collie tears through tunnels, leaps over hurdles, and scrambles up ramps, making lightning-fast twists and turns the entire way. When he darts past the finish line, an official shouts, "Time!" and all the spectators cheer.

"What is *that?*" I ask, pulling so hard on Streak's leash I'm practically choking him to keep him from shooting into the ring.

Luke's eyes are as big as jawbreakers. "Aw...I've read about this. They call it agility training. It's the hottest thing now with dogs. Owners train their dogs to run through all these obstacles, and they compete with each other to see who goes the fastest and makes the fewest mistakes. Look," he says, pointing to the group of contestants. "Over half of them are Border collies. I'll bet Streak would do great at this."

I look down at Streak and try to imagine it. But when I look up, my head spins.

"Hi, Guy! Hi, Luke and Streak."

"C-Catherine," I gasp. She's the last person I expect to see here. Her cheeks are pink in the brisk temperatures, and they match the purple corduroy pants and wool winter coat she's wearing. Big white snowflakes land like diamonds on her brown hair, and her green eyes sparkle as they peer at me through her enormous red-rimmed glasses.

"Wh-what are you doing here?" I ask, my heart doing a swing dance.

"My sister is showing our Jack Russell terrier today and I came up for moral support."

"Oh."

"I also thought it would be fun to watch Streak in the Frisbee contest. Are you ready?"

My spirit rebounds. "Oh yeah. We're ready," I say, noticing that Luke has drifted off for a closer look at the other dogs.

Catherine kneels down to scratch Streak under his chin. "He looks ready," she tells me. "You've done a great job with him."

Suddenly the day is feeling a lot warmer. "It's mostly Luke," I tell her, at the same time realizing this is the longest conversation we've ever had.

"Have you finished reading *Fahrenheit 451*?"

"Uh, no. Not yet." I'm about to make up some excuse,

but decide to be honest. "I've been too worried about the contest and other stuff."

"Yeah, I know how that is," Catherine says. "I wouldn't have read it either if I had something like this coming up. Anyway, good luck today. I'll be rooting for you."

"Uh, thanks," I stammer. "Good luck to you, too. I mean, to your sister."

Catherine smiles and walks away.

I hope I didn't sound like too much of an idiot.

* * *

With all the action going on, two o'clock arrives faster than a good butt sniff. Luke, my mom, and I take Streak to the contest area, a big field now covered in three inches of snow. Streak is going crazy. It's not just the big crowd and the forty or so other dogs milling around. This is the first time he's ever been in snow and he loves it. He jumps up and down and shoves his nose in it and flicks it up in the air. If I didn't have him on a leash, he'd be roaring around like a snowmobile.

I keep an eye out for Brad Mullen, but I don't see him anywhere. As Luke and I step up to the registration table, though, I smell a familiar gaseous odor.

"Glad you could make it, Calf Crap."

I turn to see Brad and Shep breathing down my neck. I thought I'd gotten over my fear of this guy, but the rock in my throat corrects me.

"Where are your goons?" I ask, trying to sound as

brave as possible. "Didn't their mommies let them come?"

Brad's eyes flash and his fists clench, but he doesn't dare do anything in this crowd.

"Name?" a man behind the table asks.

I turn away from Brad. "Guy Martinez."

"Dog's name?"

"Streak."

The man checks a list and then asks, "You here for the qualifying round?"

"Yes sir."

"Okay, we'll be starting in a few minutes."

The man motions to a pile of white Frisbees. "These are the official discs. You can use any one you want, but I suggest you take a couple and get used to them before the contest. Have fun out there."

"Thanks," I say.

As Luke and I turn away, Brad Mullen whispers, "Take good care of my dog for me." At first I'm confused, thinking he means Shep. Then I realize he's talking about Streak. Luke pulls me away.

"Come on. Let's practice with these Frisbees."

Brad snickers and steps up to the table to register.

* * *

Luke and I go find my mom. She's brought our camera and I make sure she's in a good position to catch the action. Then I tell her we're going to go practice before the contest starts.

"Good luck, all of you. Remember, it doesn't matter if you win or not. Just have a good time."

As we're walking away, Luke says, "I guess you didn't tell her about the bet?"

I shake my head. "Are you crazy? I didn't want to get her upset. I'm upset enough for both of us."

We reach an empty part of the field. I try to get into Frisbee mode, but I can still feel myself fuming.

Luke must feel it too. "Don't think about Brad," he tells me. "Just remember to relax and throw like we've been practicing." He unclips Streak from his leash and he goes blasting through the snow.

"Here, Streak!" I say, waving the Frisbee around. After a couple of snowy nose-shoves, Streak trots back to me. I cock my arm and throw. The Frisbee is lighter than the ones we've been practicing with, which makes it easier to toss, but harder to control. It zips out of my hand, but then does a quick right turn and plunges into the snow before Streak can reach it.

"I don't like these Frisbees," I tell Luke.

Luke is holding one of the discs in his left hand, and tugging on his earlobe with his right. "Aw...I see what you mean. I'll bet these are the same kind they had in the city championships—"

"Which means Brad and Shep have been practicing with the right Frisbees and we've been practicing with the wrong ones."

"Shoot. You're right." Luke sounds concerned for a split-second, but his natural optimism bursts through. "That's okay, though. You're better at throwing than

Brad, and Streak's better at catching than Shep. You'll be able to make the adjustment. Just remember, don't get greedy and try to reach the 40-yard line. Aim for the 30 and you'll do great."

I toss the Frisbee again, but not as hard. It's tricky getting the disc to fly flat without diving off to one side, but after a few throws, both Streak and I are getting the hang of it. I'm still not totally comfortable, but after one more throw, the whistle blows.

It's now or never.

Chapter Seventeen

S treak and I make it through the qualifying round with a few points to spare, scoring an 11.5. I'm not happy with my performance, but by the end I'm getting the feel of the new Frisbees.

"I hope I do better in the real contest," I tell Luke afterward.

"You will. All that matters now is that we're in."

The organizers assign the owner-dog teams at random and we're given one of the last slots in the competition. Number 32. As the competition starts, the weather is worrying me as much as the new Frisbees.

By the time the first owner-dog pair steps up to the throwing line, the snow is falling in curtains. I've never seen anything like it except in movies, and I'm pretty amazed by the whole thing. There's no doubt that it's going to make the competition even more challenging. Usually there are white lines marking the 10-, 20-, 30-, and 40-yard distances, but the snow's obliterated those. Today, all we've got to go on are big orange cones along the sidelines.

The snow doesn't seem to bother anyone else. It's just another Montana day for most people and everyone cheerfully gabs and plays with their dogs as the contest gets underway.

The first dog up scores an impressive 13.5 points. The second dog gets 10 and the third, 15.5.

"Aw...this isn't like the other contests," Luke says.

"No," I agree. "These dogs are better."

Having slot 32 gives Luke, Streak, and me a lot of time to sit around being nervous. I glance through the crowd and spot Brad and Shep pacing back and forth. They ended up with slot 33, right behind us, and Brad looks like he's as anxious to get going as we are. I also see Catherine and our eyes meet. She gives me a little wave and I return it.

"What do you think about Catherine?" I ask Luke.

His every neuron is focused on the dogs. "What do you mean?"

"I don't know," I say, regretting that I asked. "Just what do you think about her?"

"You mean does she like you?"

The flush of heat melts the snowflakes on my face. "*No.* I mean..."

What do I mean?

"I think you should talk to her more," Luke says, and returns his attention to the dogs.

I sigh and do the same. Dog #16 scores 15 points. Dog #22 scores a dismal 4. Dog #27 scores 12. So far the high score of the day is 17 points by a dog named Windmill. Windmill is a medium-height dog about the size of Streak. Also like Streak, she has a docked tail, but her coloring is white with big splotches of brown. As Windmill runs, her legs seem to flail in all directions. But geez, can she catch a Frisbee!

"She's a springer spaniel," Luke tells me. "They're usually hunting dogs, but they're really strong and pretty fast. I never thought of them catching Frisbees, but I guess it makes sense."

Windmill's owner is a tall, overweight man who looks like a trucker or professional beer-drinker. He seems like the last person who would have a great Frisbee dog, but he knows what he's doing. I overhear someone next to me say that Windmill finished third in the national Frisbee contest the previous year. I can see why. The big guy and Windmill operate like clockwork. The man sails the Frisbee out just past the 30-yard mark and Windmill flails after it, usually catching the disc a good three or four feet off the ground before racing back to the throw line. Only once does Windmill catch it on the ground and fail to get the half-point bonus. They look ridiculous, but they're good.

"Windmill's going to be hard to beat," Luke tells me and I know he's thinking the same thing I am.

During our practice sessions we've never tried to throw it out beyond the 40-yard mark, and the reasons are obvious. Even though you get an astounding 5 points for a 40-yard throw—5.5 if your dog catches it in the air—your reliability goes way down. So most people aim for the 30-yard mark. But then along come Windmill and his owner, who have already scored about the maximum possible at the 30-yard distance and look like they could throw 40 yards in the next round. Worse, I know from the Fall Fair that Brad is also strong enough to clear the 40-yard line. Luke and I have discounted this before, thinking he'd never be able to pull that off again, but now I'm having second thoughts.

If Brad believes that 40 yards is what it will take to win, I think, *he might just get lucky and pull it off.*

"What do you think I should do?" I ask Luke. "I don't care about beating Windmill, but I *have* to beat Brad. Should I try for the 40-yard mark?"

Suddenly the announcer shouts, "Guy Martinez and Streak!"

My heart—or maybe it's my spleen—leaps up and tries to pop out of my mouth, but I force it back down.

Luke looks at me. "Aw...I don't know, Guy. Can you even throw it forty yards?"

"I'm not sure. Maybe on a good day. I wish Brad had gone ahead of us so we would know what we're dealing with."

"Yeah," Luke agrees. He thinks for another moment, but doesn't come up with any revelations. Finally he leans over and whispers to Streak. "Go get 'em, boy!" Then to me he says, "I guess just throw it the way you think is best."

Big help.

I take a deep breath and, without knowing what I'm going to do, make my way through the crowd. Off to the side I see Brad Mullen sneer and flip me off. I also see my mom making her way to one of the 20-yard orange cones, her camera at the ready. She waves, but I don't wave back.

"Is this Streak?" the starter asks.

I nod.

"You understand the rules? You get one minute to throw as many times as you can. You'll get another chance in Round Two. High score counts, but if I were you, I'd do my best this time. This snow is only going to get worse."

"Okay," I say, my tongue barely working. I bend down to unclip Streak from his lead. For a second I'm afraid he's just going to start playing in the snow, but he seems to sense this is the real thing. He shoots out about five yards and then spins around to stare at the disc in my hand.

"Ready!" the starter yells.

Streak and I both tense.

"Set!"

Streak does a quick 360.

"Go!"

I fling the Frisbee straight out. It sails smoothly beyond the 30-yard mark. It curves slightly to the right, but it's not too far, not too short. Streak easily chases it down and leaps, bagging the Frisbee in midair for 3.5 points. A few whoops go up from the crowd, but it's like I'm hearing them underwater. All my attention zeroes in on Streak as he comes racing back to me, kicking up snow behind him.

I take the Frisbee from him and throw it again. The throw is much like the last one, not too hard, but just far enough to clear the 30-yard mark. Streak again hunts it down with a smooth leap into the air. The crowd cheers a little louder. Now we've got 7 points.

I throw the Frisbee again and Streak performs like I've never seen him. Snow spotting his fur like white polka dots, he nails the Frisbee as if he's the only real competitor out there. Before I know it, we've got 10.5 points. But we're only partway there.

"Fifteen seconds to go!" the starter yells.

As I take the Frisbee from Streak one more time, I realize that we've got time for two more throws—and a chance at the lead. I swing my arm back and decide to again throw for the 30-yard line. It's a good throw and Streak starts after it. But just then a loud two-note whistle cuts through the noise of the crowd. The whistle is exactly like the one I use to get Streak's attention. Streak screeches to a halt and looks at the crowd and then at me, his ears at full alert.

"Go!" I yell, motioning to the Frisbee. After a split second, Streak bounds after it, but it's too late. The Frisbee plows into the snow.

"Come on!" I yell, and Streak picks up the disc and rushes back to me. I pull it out of his mouth, but we've lost too much time. As I swing my arm back to throw, the starter shouts "Time!"

A few people clap, but I hear a lot more mumbling.

I pat Streak on the head. "Good boy!" I tell him, but my pulse is pounding as Luke walks up to me.

"What happened?" Luke asks, giving Streak a dog treat.

"That's what I want to know," I say, still dazed.

"Next dog!" the starter yells. "Brad Mullen and Shep!"

The crowd parts for Brad and his German shepherd and we're face to face. "Step aside, losers," Brad says with a smirk.

In that instant I know what happened. There's only one person here besides Luke who knows the whistle I use to call Streak—at least, only one person who'd use it against me.

I start to say something, but the words stick in my throat. Brad laughs and says, "Watch how it's done!"

I glare at Brad, fire burning in my chest.

"He did it," I tell Luke.

Luke looks at me. "Are you sure? He whistled at Streak?"

"I'm sure. He heard me use that whistle at the Fall Fair."

"Ready!" the starter yells for Brad.

"What are you going to do?" Luke asks me.

"I'm not sure," I say.

"Set!" the starter yells.

Brad pulls his arm back with the Frisbee.

"Go!"

I watch as Brad throws the Frisbee for Shep. I feel like going out there and kicking Brad in the butt as he's about to throw, but I don't. And I have to admit that he and Shep are good. Brad throws the Frisbees just about perfect. Most of his throws clear the 30-yard line, but one clears the 40. Fortunately, the snow slows down Shep enough that he has to catch them on the ground, but still, their performance is impressive.

"Time!" the starter yells. "Brad and Shep—17 points!"

The crowd claps. Brad and Shep are now in a dead heat for first place and my brain churns over what I should do about it. I can go tell the judges what Brad did and try to get him disqualified, but it would be hard to prove. I can also do something equally rotten to Brad, but that's not my style. I want to win this thing straight out.

As the final few dogs compete, I scramble for a plan.

Chapter Eighteen

By the time the second round starts, snow is coming down in big chunks. The judges confer about whether to continue the match, but none of the dog owners show any sign of leaving, so the contest continues. For Round Two, the dogs compete in the reverse order. This is good for Streak and me since we'll go sooner instead of later, when conditions might even be worse. But it also means that I've got to move fast.

"So," Luke asks, "did you decide what you're going to do?"

I nod. "I think so. Listen, Luke. Do me a favor and go tell the judge over there to keep an eye on Brad when Streak and I are up."

"Aw...sure. What should I say?"

"Tell him you thought you saw Brad whistle during the last round and you want to make sure it'll be a fair competition."

Luke grins. "Okay. I like that." He walks off and I scan the crowd for Brad. I see him off to the side by himself, and Streak and I head toward him. As I approach, I go over what I'm going to say.

"Hey, loser!" Brad says. I feel like knocking his smirk right off his face, but I stay calm.

"Big score," I say. "Too bad you had to cheat to get it."

Shep strains toward Streak, wagging his tail, but Brad tugs him back.

"I don't know what you're talking about," he tells me.

I force a laugh. "Yeah, sure. You cheat at everything, Brad. Math, English, you even cheat with friends. I just thought you'd at least be honest where your dog's concerned."

Brad's fake smile turns down and he steps forward menacingly. "You want a busted face?"

I keep grinning, even though I feel like a cherry bomb with a lit fuse. "What's really the matter?" I ask. "Are you afraid you can't do anything unless you cheat?"

"I can win this contest hands down."

"Is that right," I say, drooling sarcasm.

"Yeah!"

"Well, you're going to have to from now on. I've got three witnesses who saw you whistle and if you try it again, I'll turn you in." I pause to let that sink in. "I may turn you in anyway."

"You've got nothing," Brad says, but I see doubt cross his face.

"I do, and I've told the judge to watch you, just in case."

"You little bastard."

This is basically what I've been waiting for. My plan is to get Brad riled up and then drop the hammer on him by saying something insulting about his dead father. Payback. Tit for tat. I figure that between his anger and his fear, it might just throw his Frisbee-tossing out of balance—which is my best shot at getting a fair round. As I open my mouth to deliver the blow, though, I lock onto Brad's eyes and suddenly I change my mind. As much as I despise this moron, I also know what it's like to lose a father. I just can't bring myself to rub salt in this particular wound, no matter what Brad's already done to me.

But that doesn't mean I can't say *something*.

"Well, we'll see," I say, stepping away. "I hope you're feeling strong, though. With this cold air, you're going to have to throw the Frisbee a lot harder to get it out beyond the 30-yard line."

"Yeah, right, Calf Crap," Brad snorts.

"Fine, don't believe me," I tell him. "But lower temperatures make air denser and harder to move through. Every 5-degree drop in temperature makes the air 50 percent heavier. You'll probably have to throw the Frisbee 75 percent harder to make up for it."

Brad looks at me suspiciously and says, "You're full of it." Which is totally true. Air is denser when it's cold, but I'm just making up the part about having to throw harder. Still, I'm almost positive Brad doesn't know that.

"Well, let's see if you're right," he says, picking up a Frisbee.

"Go ahead," I say, shrugging. "You'll see."

But before Brad can throw, the starter calls his name. "Brad Mullen and Shep—you're on deck!"

"Good luck," I say, leading Streak away. "You'll need it."

Brad looks at me, his lips pressed together like a Ziploc bag.

* * *

By the time Brad steps up to the line, at least six inches of snow cover the ground—enough for smaller dogs to trip or stumble in. Shep's so massive he can plow through it, but when Brad pulls back to make his first throw, he heaves the Frisbee way too hard and it goes wild. It careens left, dives into the snow, and rolls toward the sideline. Shep doesn't even get close and it takes him twice the usual time to retrieve it.

Luke and I grin and give each other a high five. It looks as if my physics lesson on the density of gases is working.

On the next throw, Brad overcompensates and Shep—all set for another long heave—actually overruns the Frisbee. Again it falls into the snow.

After that, Brad gets the distance more or less right, but I can tell he's rattled. When the starter yells "Time!" Brad's completed only three successful throws for 9 points. I only have a moment to enjoy Brad's bungle, though. Streak and I are up next, and we need 17.5 points to beat Brad and Windmill—and *that* will only be enough if no one does better. My nerves dancing like the swirling snowflakes, I take Streak up to the line and unhook his lead.

"Just take a deep breath and throw like normal,"

Luke says from behind me. I glance over at one of the judges to see that he's watching Brad, and that makes me feel a little better. Before I know it, the starter shouts, "Go!"

The next sixty seconds pass like a blur. I'm in an altered state, like my mind's been abducted by aliens. I throw. Streak brings it back. I throw. Streak brings it back again. I worry that the snow is going to slow him down, but it seems to energize him instead. His slender, horselike legs whip through the flakes like foam, one throw after another. Three, four, five times—the last one almost reaching the 40-yard mark. By the time the starter calls time, I have no idea how many points we have, but Luke rushes up to us and yells, "You did it!"

The fog lifts from my brain. "We did?"

"Aw...yeah! 17 points exactly—and if Streak had nabbed that last one in the air, you'd have the outright lead!"

It's not the unqualified victory I was looking for, but it gives me new life.

"Oh, man," I say, bending down to give Streak a hug. "Way to go, boy!"

"Now all we have to do is hope nobody does any better," Luke says.

I take a deep breath. "Yeah."

We don't have to worry. Streak's one of the only dogs that does better in the second round than in the first. Even Windmill the Wonder Dog scores only 14 on his second run. After the last dog scrambles through the snow, the judges compare the highest scores from each

155

round. The starter announces, "Congratulations on all of the fine performances by dogs and owners today. Especially in such, um, unusual conditions."

The crowd laughs and claps.

"After judging all the scores, it looks as like we've got a three-way tie for first place. In just a moment, we'll have a throw-off between Windmill, Shep, and Streak. And their owners, of course."

Everyone again laughs. Luke looks at me. "Are you ready?"

I look down at Streak. "I guess we'd better be."

Chapter Nineteen

By the luck of the draw, Streak and I go first. At least seven or eight inches of snow cover the ground and it's falling so thickly I can barely see the orange cones marking the 40-yard line. Not a single person has left, however. Every one of the owners and dogs—not to mention about a hundred spectators and two local TV crews—has crowded around the snow-covered sidelines.

"Are you all set?" the starter asks.

For the fourth time that day I nod and let Streak off his lead. He dashes out in front of me and I worry whether he'll even be able to see the white Frisbee in this blizzard.

"Go get 'em!" Luke yells.

Then I hear a familiar voice. "Go, Guy!"

I turn to see Catherine in the crowd about twenty-five feet away. She smiles and I can't help myself. I smile back.

Immediately after that, I hear an exaggerated choking sound behind me. I know who it is, but I've come too far to let Brad get to me now.

"Ready!" the starter yells.

I shake out my arms and pull the Frisbee back. Streak tenses, leaning to one side. Puffs of steam shoot out of his open, eager mouth, and his black legs quiver like they've got rocket fuel in them, just waiting for the command to launch.

"Set!... *Go!*"

I release the Frisbee and Streak blasts toward it. It's a good throw, easily clearing the 30-yard line. Streak snatches it out of the air before making a quick U-turn back toward me. A few people clap.

The second throw also goes well, and so does the third. When Streak comes rushing back to me, we're up to 10.5 points. But I can see that Streak is having to bound through the deeper snow instead of just running through it, and that's starting to slow him down. For the fourth throw, I decide to loft it a little higher to give him more time to get under it.

Mistake.

I throw the Frisbee too high and it stalls and slips back. Streak is already beyond the 30-yard line, but now he has to turn and dive back toward the Frisbee. He just misses and I hear the crowd gasp.

As Streak grabs the Frisbee and gallops back to me, I try to pull myself together.

"That's okay, Streak," I tell him, but I'm really telling myself.

I decide to throw just like I did before. I cock back my arm and fling the Frisbee toward the 30-yard cones. The entire crowd hushes as Streak tears after it. The only noise is the sound of his heaving breath and his legs churning through the snow. The disc reaches its peak and then smoothly descends, crossing the 30-yard mark. I'm not sure it's going to be high enough for Streak to nab the bonus, but he gives it a heroic effort, leaping at the last possible moment. His feet barely clear the ground and he drags down the disc for a final 3.5 points.

"Time!" the starter yells.

Everyone around me claps—everyone except Brad, of course. I squat down and pet Streak, who's happily wagging his stump but obviously wants me to keep throwing the Frisbee. "Good boy!" I tell him.

Luke comes up to me. "Aw...that was good," he says. "14 points. Way to go."

But I can tell he and I are thinking the same thing. And for the first time that day, I'm forced to face the unthinkable. I might actually lose this contest to Brad Mullen—and lose our bet, too.

Luke and I walk back into the crowd. "I blew it," I say.

"No, you didn't."

"Yeah. I did. I just thought that with the snow so thick..."

"It's alright. The other dogs are going to have just as hard a time in this stuff as you did."

"I don't know, Luke. What am I going to do if Brad beats us?"

Just then my mom appears. "That was *great!*" she tells us. "You and Streak were wonderful!"

"Uh, thanks, Mom," I say. She still has no idea what this contest is really about.

She gives Streak a pat, but fortunately resists kissing me in front of everyone. Then she backs up and says, "How about a photo of Team Streak all together?"

Luke and I stand on either side of Streak and I force a smile, which is difficult with my gut twisting like a tornado. *If Mom only knew what was going on,* I think, *she wouldn't look nearly so proud of us. Of me,* I correct myself. I breathe a sigh of relief when she slogs off through the snow again so she can get a good view of the final two contestants. Whatever happens, I don't want her around for the outcome, especially because I have no idea what I'm going to do next.

I look down at Streak and am again overcome with guilt. Can I really even think about turning him over to Brad Mullen? I've been taught to keep my word and all that, but now I have to decide. Do I care more about keeping my word to a bully or to my dog?

* * *

The starter calls Windmill and her owner next. Luke and I move closer to watch. I want to laugh every time I look at Windmill. Her name matches her perfectly. "She looks like a dog designed by an engineer," I tell Luke.

He laughs. "You're right. Look at those legs and ears."

But Windmill's loaded with talent. When the starter yells, "Go!" she flails through the snow like a high-speed hydroplane. A white cloud kicks up behind her and she zooms in on the Frisbee like she's got radar.

The spectators love it and there's no doubt she's the favorite. Again and again her giant owner tosses the disc. Again and again she chases it down. When they're finished, they've racked up 17.5 points—perfect for the 30-yard distance, and in today's conditions, pretty much unbeatable.

"Aw...so much for the trophy," Luke says.

"Yeah," I say, but I couldn't care less about the trophy. All I care about is who's up next.

"Brad Mullen and Shep!" the starter yells.

Brad squeezes by Luke and me, then stops and spits. "Say good-bye to your dog," he hisses.

Our eyes lock for what seems like a geological era. I see the usual malice in Brad's eyes, but I also see just a hint of fear. I feel like I should say something, but can think of nothing.

"Brad and Shep!" the starter repeats.

"Look and learn, Calf Crap," Brad says and takes Shep up to the line. All eyes are on them, even Streak's.

Brad unhitches Shep from his leash and mutters something to him. Shep wags his tail and for the first time I realize that maybe Brad actually cares about his dog. I don't know why that surprises me so much, but it does.

"Ready!" the starter shouts. "Set! Go!"

The TV cameras point at Shep as Brad pulls back and lets the Frisbee fly. The throw is perfect. Shep plows after it and somehow even manages to leap into the air to catch it.

Three and a half points.

I guess my psychological warfare wore off, I think.

Shep races back, the Frisbee in his mouth. Brad rips it loose and throws it again. Again, the throw is perfect. Shep doesn't leap this time, but easily traps it between his jaws.

Six and a half points.

A panic begins rising in me, but I push it down. Brad can't possibly keep this up...can he?

Brad throws again—this time a monster beyond the 40-yard mark. I'm amazed he would try that under these conditions, but Shep gives it his all and bags it just before it hits the ground.

Eleven and a half points.

"Aw," Luke mutters. "I can't watch."

I feel the same way. As Shep comes racing back toward Brad, panic explodes through me, making me feel weak and dizzy. *Man,* I think, *they are really in a groove.* My head swirls as I realize that they're not only going to win our bet, they're going to win the entire contest. I just can't believe this is happening. As Brad pulls the Frisbee from Shep's mouth, he looks at me and we both know. One more throw and he wins the bet—and Streak.

"Fifteen seconds!" calls the starter.

Brad pulls back his arm and lets the Frisbee go. I hold my breath. The throw is beautiful, out near the 40-yard mark, and Shep bounds after it, snowflakes swirling all around him. In my mind I can see him launching off the ground, rising toward the descending Frisbee, and seizing it in his jaws.

Only he doesn't.

Instead of grabbing the Frisbee, Shep comes to an abrupt stop. He turns toward Brad and wags his tail, letting the disc fall into the snow next to him.

The crowd turns stone still. Luke and I look at each other, then back at Shep.

"Shep!" Brad screams. "Frisbee!"

Shep again wags his tail and drops his front legs into a crouch.

"He's playing!" Luke utters in astonishment. "Shep's playing a game!"

"You're right!" I gasp.

"Shep!" Brad yells, sounding like a hysterical chicken. He races out toward his dog and Shep dodges him playfully. Brad swears and scoops up the Frisbee. "Shep! Come!" he yells, running back to the throw line. Shep bounds after him, kicking up powder, obviously having a great time.

Brad pulls his arm back, but it's all over.

"Time!" the starter yells.

The crowd erupts into clapping, laughing, shouting, and hooting.

Luke and I again look at each other.

"I can't believe it!" I say.

"Wow!" Luke holds up his hand for a high five and I swing to slap it, but miss. We both crack up.

The TV crews swarm around Windmill and her owner, and soon Streak, Luke, and I have our own crowd. All these people start congratulating me and trying to pet Streak. I don't have the faintest idea who most of them are, but I do recognize a couple of classmates. Catherine is one of them and I try to talk to her, but I'm so jostled and shocked and relieved by everything that I barely manage to say hi. Twenty minutes later, though, as Luke and I pull Streak from the crowd and walk back to the car, Catherine's face still sticks to my mind like fresh-fallen snow.

Chapter Twenty

That night, we end up staying in Missoula. By evening the storm has dropped over eleven inches of snow—the most in a decade, according to the local news. Luke says that even with a four-wheel drive, we'd have trouble getting back to Coffee. So my mom checks us into a place called the Creekside Motel, and that evening we trudge downtown to an old theater called The Wilma. The theater needs a total overhaul, but Mom loves it. She says it has character. To celebrate our "victory," she buys us tickets to a new Will Smith movie, complete with popcorn and drinks.

The next day the storm passes, and as soon as the roads are cleared we head back to Coffee. We drop off Luke and then listen to our tires crunch over the snow as Mom steers towards Grandpa's house. When we arrive, Grandpa is outside with a shovel, trying to dig out the driveway.

"Hey, how are the local heroes?" Grandpa shouts when we pile out of the car. "You and Streak made page three of the sports section today!"

"Really?" I ask him, surprised. "But we only came in second."

"Second's good enough for Coffee," Grandpa says. "Congratulations, boy."

After Grandpa and my mom go inside, I pick up the snow shovel and keep working on the driveway. Shoveling snow is another first for me and I find that I enjoy it. Each time I fling a shovelful, Streak leaps into the air and tries to bite it. I laugh watching him, and it makes the work go a lot quicker.

As I lift and toss the scoops of snow into a pile along the driveway, though, I feel jumpy, off balance, and at first can't figure out what it's from. I thought that after Streak and I beat Brad in the Frisbee contest, everything would be okay. Brad would be off my back and maybe I could start trying to have a normal life around here. But the higher the white wall along the driveway gets, the more I feel that something's not quite right.

* * *

The next morning, I walk to school early. Instead of going to the front entrance, I head for the Smoking Tree a half a block away. Sure enough, Brad and the Parasites are there, chewing and puffing away. Brad scowls as I approach, but he seems to be missing some of his usual "bad attitude."

"What do you want?" he says.

"I want to talk to you. Alone."

He spits. "What for?"

"Just for a minute," I say and take a few steps away from the tree.

"No kissing," Harold Dicks says with a cackle. Brad punches him in the shoulder and pain twists his face. Satisfied he's re-established the pecking order, Brad follows me, chewing a wad of Red Man.

"What is it, Calf Crap? Don't even think about—"

"Look, Brad," I say, talking low enough so the others can't hear. "I just wanted to tell you a couple of things."

Brad keeps his tough face on, but I see a spark of curiosity.

"First," I say, "I thought you and Shep did real well Saturday. It was only luck that we beat you."

"You don't think I know that?"

"Second," I say, feeling the tightness in my voice, "I know I won the bet, but you don't have to shave your head—or Shep's either."

Brad stops chewing and spits. "Like I was going to anyways."

The comment doesn't totally surprise me, but makes me pause.

"That it?" Brad says.

"No. There's one more thing. I don't want you torturing the kids around here next year."

"Yeah?" Brad asks, starting to chew again. "Who's going to stop me? You and your lame-ass friend?"

I realize how my last sentence came out and try to put it another way. "What I mean," I tell him, "is next year could be different for you. You need help in math. That's something I'm good at. I could help you get through it."

"I don't need your damn help," Brad says.

"We can keep it quiet," I say. "It'll be just between you and me. Luke doesn't even have to know."

Brad pulls out his tobacco pouch and places a fresh pinch in his mouth. He glances off at the distant mountains and then back at me. Finally he asks, "What do you get out of it?"

"Well," I tell him. "It'll be just as easy working on math with you as by myself. Also, I don't like you and I'm sure you don't like me—"

"You got that right."

"—but no one should have to hang around middle school their entire life. Even you."

Brad chews a few times and spits at a nearby cola can. He hits it dead on. Then he repeats, "That it?"

I nod. Brad returns to the Parasites, and I walk back toward the front of the school to meet Luke. The twist in my stomach is gone.

* * *

Things move pretty fast after that. Mrs. Minneman hands our *Animal Farm* papers back and I am amazed to find a B- on mine. Next to the grade she's written, "Writing needs work, but very thoughtful. Good job."

The weekend after the regional Frisbee competition, my mom drives Luke, Streak, and me to the State Frisbee Championships in Helena. Since Streak and I finished second in Regionals, we've qualified to compete for the State Championship and the local paper does another story about us going. As expected,

Windmill wins the State title for the second year in a row, but we all have a good time. Streak and I finish eleventh out of a field of twenty, and I'm happy with that. But I think it'll be our last official competition. Luke's father told me that lots of dogs get injured jumping and twisting to catch Frisbees and I don't want Streak to end up crippled. Besides, I realize I have just as much fun playing with Streak in the backyard as I do competing.

With the end of the Frisbee contests, I expect life to percolate back into the usual slow Coffee routine, but it doesn't. Just before the Thanksgiving holidays, Mom comes home and says, "I have a special proclamation."

I think she's going to tell me that we're moving back to California or she's gotten a promotion at work or something. Instead, she announces that she's leased a corner shop downtown and has decided to open a combination coffee bar and bookstore.

"I'm calling it 'The Coffee Place'," she tells Grandpa and me. "Get it? Isn't that clever?"

"But how—"

"Grandpa here generously took out a loan on the house," Mom explains. "After we get The Coffee Place fixed up and opened, we have about six months to start making a profit."

"And then?" I ask her.

Mom chuckles. "Who knows? Six months seems like a lifetime right now. Who can predict farther than that?"

Looking back at my own last six months in Coffee, I can see her point. But what it means is that from then until Christmas, Luke and I spend weekends, afternoons, and vacation days helping her and a bunch of contractors get the place in shape. Mom prints up flyers with coupons offering a 10 percent discount, and we hand them out all over town. We finally get the new books on the shelves on December 20, the night before the grand opening, and the shop looks pretty spiff. The next morning—winter solstice—I'm amazed what a hit The Coffee Place is. Mom puts Luke to work restocking shelves and helping people find books, and I operate the cash register. Man, people just pack the place. They gulp down gallons of espressos, mochas, and lattes and buy hundreds of dollars worth of books.

"Can you believe this?" I ask Luke. "Where'd all these people come from?"

"I don't know, but they're sure buying a lot of books."

"And drinking a lot of coffee."

"Don't expect it to keep going like this," Mom tells us one evening after we close up, and she's right. After the Grand Opening and the Christmas shopping rush, things slow down a bit—but not nearly as much as she predicts. I'd always thought of Coffee as a hick town, but it turns out to have a lot more variety than I ever realized. Hippies, New Agers, bankers—just about every type of person you can think of—all start hanging out at The Coffee Place. I don't know anything about business, but even I can see that Mom's store is probably going to make it.

* * *

All this time I've pushed the possibility of Luke moving away to the back of my mind. Luke hasn't said anything more about it and with each passing day I figure it's that much more likely that he and his folks will decide to stay. One day, after work, though, Luke drops the bomb.

"We're moving to Portland next week," he tells me. The lead weight returns to my stomach, and I can see by the look on his face that he feels just as lousy as I do.

"Is it for sure?" I ask.

Luke nods. "Aw...yeah. My parents put our house on the market yesterday. Dad says we'll rent a place in Portland until the house here sells."

He tells me that his dad has decided to start a new veterinary practice after all, but his parents just need a change and want to get out of Coffee. It sounds all too familiar to me, but I try not to show my disappointment.

"But did I tell you?" Luke says. "My parents said I can get a dog again. Maybe even two."

I smile. "That's great." If there's anyone who should have a dog—or maybe even a hundred of them—it's Luke.

My mom suggests we invite Luke and his family over for a little farewell dinner before they leave. She makes her famous baked macaroni and cheese and after we finish eating, Luke and I throw the ball for Streak one last time. In the backyard, we talk about how maybe we can visit each other in the summer. We also promise to write and e-mail each other, but it doesn't make us feel much better. Before Luke goes, I give him a photo Mom took of Streak catching a Frisbee at the regional contest in Missoula. He wipes his eyes and mutters, "Thanks." We shake hands and I feel stupid and sad doing it. What I really want to do is make him stay here, but I know I can't. He has to go and I have to stay and suck it up.

* * *

The only thing that helps me feel less awful about Luke leaving is I've got lots of work to keep me busy. When classes start up again after New Year's, The Coffee Place starts becoming a regular hangout for students from my school and the high school. They pour in every afternoon after last period and I've got to race to keep up with all the orders and clean off the tables. I also try to pay special attention to one particular customer.

Almost every day Catherine and her friends come in and sit in the same seats. Pretty soon I make a Reserved sign for their table to make sure no one else takes their spot. When the after-school rush slows down, I casually amble my way over there. We chat about classes, books, music, who likes who at school, and that sort of stuff. More and more, though, I notice Catherine talking to me instead of her girlfriends and once or twice, she even drops in by herself. One afternoon I get up my courage and invite her to a movie. To my surprise, she says yes. We go out that Friday night and have an even better time than I expect. After the movie, we sit at a local diner called 4 Bs and talk until almost 11:00. Afterward, I walk her home. I'm too nervous to try to kiss her or hold her hand, but I get the feeling she wouldn't mind if I did.

The next morning—Saturday—I decide to take Streak for a walk in the park near Grandpa's house. Three inches of fresh powder have fallen during the night, but the sun is out, turning Coffee into this dazzling winter wonderland.

I take a tennis ball with me and toss it for Streak along the way, thinking of Catherine and what a good time we had the night before. When I reach the park, though, I see someone throwing a Frisbee for his dog. It's Brad and Shep.

For a moment, I consider turning around and finding a different park. Brad and I haven't said a word to each other since our conversation at the Smoking Tree and that's been fine with me. He's stopped bullying me, but he never did ask for help with math and to tell you the truth, I never expected him to. I'm happy just having him out of my life and I'm guessing he feels the same way.

But today we're the only two people anywhere in sight and it would seem way too obvious for me to turn around and walk away. Instead I suck the twenty-degree air into my lungs and shuffle through the powder up to Brad.

He glances at me, but quickly returns his eyes to Shep, who's bounding back to him with a yellow Frisbee in his mouth.

I throw the ball for Streak and say, "How's it going?"

Brad grunts, but I can't tell if any real words come out. He takes the Frisbee from Shep and tosses it again. Shep bounds after it and catches it, and before I can stop him, Streak tears after him, kicking up a wave of white powder.

"Streak, come!" I call.

Streak ignores me and grabs Shep's Frisbee right out of his mouth. I expect Brad to get mad, but he doesn't. The dogs are soon ripping through the snow, having a great game of chase and steal-the-Frisbee. It's not the first time Streak has shown me that dogs sometimes have more sense than people do, and I decide to try and follow his example.

"Shep's looking real good," I tell Brad. "You must have been working him a lot."

I see a bit of pride show through on Brad's face. "Yep. We're going to kick your butt in the Frisbee contest next year."

"Did you see that agility training in Missoula?"

A grin escapes from Brad's face before he can pull it back. "Yeah. That was cool."

"You ever think of doing that with Shep?"

Brad's brief grin fades away and he shakes his head. "Too much work."

We fall silent again.

Then I ask, "How's school?"

"A waste of time, like always."

That about exhausts my ideas for conversation, so we both stand there watching the dogs race in crazy arcs and circles through the snow. After a couple of minutes I whistle for Streak and he reluctantly comes running. I give him a doggie treat and when Shep pants up behind him, I ask Brad if I can give Shep one, too.

Brad shrugs.

Shep wolfs down the treat and I scratch him on the head. I put Streak on his leash and say, "Well, I guess I'll see you around."

Brad tosses the Frisbee again. "Yeah."

I walk away, feeling relieved our little encounter is over. I also feel something else, but can't quite put my finger on what it is.

Streak and I head toward home and when we're about a block away from our place I spot Grandpa and Mom out front working on a snowman.

"Hey, we need some help!" Mom calls to us when we get closer. "Grandpa's out of practice."

"Speak for yourself, April," Grandpa says, gamely trying to scoop some snow together.

I've never built a snowman before and neither has Streak and it looks like fun. We jump in, rolling up the largest snowballs possible. We get a good base built and plop the torso on top of that. Then I roll up a head about the size of a bowling ball.

As Mom and I position the snowman's head on top of his body, I suddenly figure out what it was I was feeling earlier. It doesn't have to do just with Brad and the Frisbee contest, or with The Coffee Place or Catherine, either—though they're all part of it. It's just everything together and what's happened over the last six months.

Even though Luke is gone and I still miss my dad and California, what I figure out is this:

Whether I like it or not, Montana is starting to feel like home.

About the Author

SNEED B. COLLARD III is a biologist, world traveler, speaker, and author of more than fifty books for young people, including THE PRAIRIE BUILDERS, A PLATYPUS PROBABLY, and BEAKS!—all Junior Library Guild selections. He also wrote the YA novel FLASH POINT. Collard graduated with Honors in marine biology from the University of California at Berkeley and also a holds a master's degree from U.C. Santa Barbara. He now resides in Missoula, Montana, and was recently honored with the distinguished Lud Browman Award for his achievements in scientific writing. His first novel DOG SENSE was inspired by Mattie, his brilliant Frisbee-catching Border collie.

To learn more about Sneed, explore his website, *www.sneedbcollardiii.com.*